Without thinking, Rhiannon touched his cheek

Shane caught her hand and kissed it, his eyes dark with yearning. Wordlessly, he took her in his arms. As the blood began to flow hotly beneath the surface of her skin, Rhiannon traced a pattern in the thick ebony curls around his ears.

"There's only one place for me," he said at last, as though reaching a difficult decision, "and that's in your bed. I can't fight it any longer. I can't resist you."

He gathered her in his arms and carried her up the stairs, where he set her gently on the bed. She reached out for him, her lips on his face, his shoulders, his chest....

ELIZABETH OLDFIELD

submission

Harlequin Books

TORONTO • NEW YORK • LONDON
AMSTERDAM • PARIS • SYDNEY • HAMBURG
STOCKHOLM • ATHENS • TOKYO • MILAN

Harlequin Presents first edition May 1984
ISBN 0-373-10691-2

Original hardcover edition published in 1982
by Mills & Boon Limited

CHAPTER ONE

RHIANNON pulled her pass from the back pocket of her tight denim jeans and showed it to the security guard in the corridor.

'You'll need a pair of ear-plugs if you're going in there, love,' he said, nodding his grey head towards the heavy swing doors. 'It's sheer bedlam.'

'I want to see the first two or three numbers, then I'll be straight out.' She gave an amused grimace at the piercing shouts and screams which were penetrating the theatre doors. 'I think that's all I'll be able to stand.'

'What a noise! It's a wonder they're not deafened for life,' the man commented sourly. 'The chemists will be happy, though—sales of cough sweets should rocket to cure all those sore throats!'

Rhiannon laughed and the man joined in, despite himself. He didn't approve of the pop music world and the types it attracted, but this girl was a beauty, he admitted grudgingly to himself. She had great big brown eyes, a friendly smile and a mane of burnished chestnut-coloured hair. It looked natural, too, a rich glowing colour, not that dyed fiery red which so many girls sported these days.

'Are you a groupie?' he asked.

'Indeed not!'

'Sorry, I should have known you had too much style,' he apologised hurriedly. 'At my age I'm out of touch with the modern scene, and in any case you can't tell dukes from dustmen these days.'

Rhiannon smiled at him. 'I deal with the secretarial side of Submission's affairs,' she explained, 'I don't usually come on tour. It's well over a year since I watched a concert, and that's why I decided to give it a try now, to refresh my memory. I'm so used to seeing

5

the guys in ordinary, everyday life that it's hard to imagine what all the fuss is about.' The screams rose to a
crescendo. 'I'd better go in.' The guard held aside the
door, and Rhiannon stepped into the theatre. Gigantic,
mind-splitting waves of noise swept over her. Hurriedly
she thrust her fingers into her ears by way of protection,
and looked across the vast auditorium. Rows upon rows
of seats heaved with shouting teenagers, mainly girls,
but with a smattering of boys and some older folk.
The edgy feeling of feminine hysteria sent a tremor
through her slender body.

'We want Submission, we want Submission!' the fans
chanted, stamping their feet and clapping their hands.
Shrill whistles punctuated the chorus. Then the ruched,
gold satin curtains on stage billowed, and the uproar
died away, as though governed by remote control. The
audience sensed that the moment they had long been
awaiting was here, and the atmosphere tightened
palpably. The guard came in and stood beside Rhiannon.

'Might as well see what all the fuss is about,' he sighed
in mock despair. 'I hear enough of their music at home.
My daughter's mad keen on Submission, she tried to
buy a ticket, but all performances were sold out weeks
ago. You should have seen the queue, went right around
the block twice, it did! When she heard I was to be on
duty here she gave me strict instructions to remember
everything so I could report back—what the fellows
wear, the songs they sing—some hopes! I'm about as
observant as a mole. Hey, look at that!' The guard's
attention was caught by a plump girl with a ponytail in
the front row. She had leapt from her seat and was
spinning round and round before the stage, her arms
outstretched, her face uplifted, her eyes shining fever-
ishly behind owlish spectacles as she uttered high-
pitched screams of joy. 'Looks like she's in a trance,'
grumbled the guard.

Then a disembodied voice came over the microphone.
'Ladies and gentlemen, would you welcome please—
Submission!'

The theatre erupted. Girls bounced noisily in the seats, while others covered their faces with their hands, overcome by the thrill of the moment. Rhiannon watched cynically, and yet persuasively she too began to feel the electric excitement creep into her. It was foolish to be caught in the grip of expectation, she thought with a wry lift of an eyebrow; after all she knew the guys so well. Silently the satin curtains opened to reveal a darkened stage, then, unexpectedly, coloured lights began flashing—violet, pink, indigo, green, illuminating briefly the drums, a guitar, banks of amplifiers, a silver microphone, the electronic keyboard. Again darkness. There was a collective sigh from the audience. The spotlight swept fat and full to the side of the stage and the screams climaxed. Rhiannon smiled, enjoying the moment. There was the sudden flash of an explosion, billowy clouds of thick white smoke, and then they were there—three tall young men, Shane Santiago, Tony Grey and David Davies, her brother.

'Handsome devils, aren't they?' whispered the man beside her, as they strode out across the stage to thunderous applause. 'Hair's a bit too long for my taste. They look like three musketeers out for a wicked night on the town.' Rhiannon nodded her agreement. They did create a dashing image in tailored white suits and waistcoats, with vivid satin shirts of midnight blue. Their stage presence was exciting and the audience indicated their approval with screams and sighs. Shane, at six foot three the tallest of the trio, was a pace ahead of the others. While David and Tony grinned out, lapping up the admiration, he remained aloof and self-contained, ignoring the clamour as he made his way to the keyboard. 'Mean, moody and magnificent,' the pop magazines had unoriginally labelled him, and they were not far off the mark. Physically he was everything a pop fan could desire—lithe, lean-hipped and handsome, with black, curly hair, piercing blue eyes and a full sensuous mouth. The Filipino blood which mingled with his

English ancestry had given him the proud Latin look of arrogance.

'Isn't he the one who writes the music?' asked the guard as Shane bent over the keyboard and began picking out a melody.

'That's right, and he arranges their records.'

'A talented fellow. Wasn't he on the highbrow side before he joined Submission? I seem to remember something about him playing in an orchestra.'

'He trained as a classical pianist,' Rhiannon confirmed.

'Quite a switch, becoming a rock star,' the man commented wonderingly, but Rhiannon offered no further information. She had no wish to discuss Shane and his background. Instead she kept her eyes on the stage as Tony slung a highly polished guitar onto his shoulder. The thrum from his strings joined the rhythm and then a hypnotic beat was added to the sound as David wielded the drumsticks. Two girl singers, in black sequined bomber jackets and slinky silver pants, began swaying and gyrating, clapping their hands in time to the music. The instruments of the ten-member backing band swelled the sound, and the air throbbed with the relentless rhythm.

'Shane, Shane, I love you!' The plump girl in the front row, whom Rhiannon had noticed earlier, had risen from her seat to make a sudden dash for the steps at the side of the stage. Even from a distance it was easy to see that she was carried away by the excitement, for her plain face was a bright red.

'Get her, Joe,' shouted the security guard beside Rhiannon. Joe, a burly young man stationed beside the stage to reject such invaders, had already anticipated her move, and he stepped forward, blocking her path with all the finality of a brick wall. The girl hesitated. For a moment she appeared totally bemused, then the beat of the music quickened and, realising her defeat, she turned reluctantly.

'Shane, Shane!' she chanted again as she sat down in

her seat in the stalls, her fists clenched, her body straining forward as she willed the object of her attentions to
notice her, but he had ignored the entire episode. He
was engrossed in the music, his dark curly head lowered,
his expression intent as his fingers moved across the
keyboard with supple agility.

'That's the dreaded Betsy,' Rhiannon whispered to
the security guard. 'She's obsessed with Shane and is his
most ardent fan. She's continually bombarding him with
love letters and poetry.'

'Huh, and what does he think of that?' snorted the
man in disgust.

'It's wearing him down. At first he treated it lightheartedly, but now his patience is wearing thin. She
never lets up, she's always telephoning the London office
and asking to speak to him. When he's on tour she hangs
around the hotels where he stays. She's a distinct pain
in the neck. Whenever I come across anything from her
in the mail I have to intercept it, on his instructions. He
refuses to meet her or become involved in any way. He'd
have her shipped off to Siberia if he could.'

'Does she come to all the concerts?'

Rhiannon nodded, the thick, gleaming hair moving at
her shoulders. 'I believe she constantly follows
Submission around the country. I feel sorry for her in a
way, all that unrequited love!'

'Silly young fool,' said the man tersely. 'She's living
in a dream world.'

'That's Shane's opinion too.'

The music faded and the audience rose, clapping,
cheering, stamping their feet as they demanded more.
Brilliant white flashes from cameras stabbed the dim
light of the theatre. Then Tony came forward to introduce the next number. He was the lead singer and his
deep, vibrant voice held the audience silently captive as
he sang plaintively of his love and his despair. Rhiannon
gave a little sigh; the tune and the lyrics were good.
Even the grizzled man beside her appreciated the poignant beauty of the melody. 'I liked that,' he admitted, as

the last note hung on the air, 'They're better than the usual so-called musicians you get nowadays, punk rockers and such—even my missus enjoys their records, especially the last hit song. It was very romantic. They got a gold disc for it, didn't they? That Shane fellow must be very clever.'

Rhiannon gave a soft snort of impatience. Why must everyone make such a fuss about Shane all the time? David and Tony were talented musicians too, as Brad had been.

'This show is extremely professional, I'll bet it takes hours of rehearsing,' the man continued, oblivious of a tightness around her mouth.

'It does.' And a tremendous output of effort, strain and emotional energy, she thought to herself. The performance on stage appeared so fluent that it was impossible for an outsider to guess at the tensions and sheer hard work involved. The next number needed no introduction. As soon as the first familiar notes were played a mammoth cheer rang out. It was Submission's very first hit song, and Rhiannon felt a catch in her throat as the tune opened up a floodgate of memories. It had been written by Brad, and had started the group off on their heady path to popularity and fame. Brad had written most of the music in those days, but now his impact on the success of the group had almost been forgotten, she thought irritably, for Shane had taken his place, writing songs which invariably topped the charts. She swallowed hard, thinking how different it all would have been if Brad hadn't been killed. As the cheers rose again at the end of the number she turned. 'I'm off now,' she said to the guard. 'I've heard all I want to hear— 'bye!' She raised her hand in farewell, and swung away through the doors, threading along the corridors to the back of the stage. A second, younger, security guard stationed at the pass door watched appreciatively as she approached. Rhiannon produced her pass again.

'I've noticed you before,' he grinned, glancing down at the name printed on the card. 'You're not looking for a bit of action tonight, are you? I'd be happy to show you the sights of Manchester, such as they are.'

'No, thanks.'

'How about tomorrow night, then?' he persisted.

Rhiannon shook her head quickly. His admiration was a little too blatant, his eyes working their way down her shapely body as he mentally undressed her. He growled in his throat as she walked by, and Rhiannon increased her pace to avoid the hand which she knew was itching to reach out and pat her bottom. It was strange how, because she was connected with show business, albeit secondhand, everyone imagined she was flirty and flighty. If only they knew what an innocent young lady I really am! she pondered ruefully. She peered through the gloom at the side of the stage and joined a portly man in his early fifties who was rubbing his hands together gleefully as he followed the performance.

'It looks good, Eddie,' she commented, watching the moving figures on the brightly lit stage.

'Fantastic,' he beamed. 'It's been the most successful tour yet. It seems as though Submission can do no wrong, and box office receipts have broken all records.' He took his eyes off the stage for a moment. 'I want to thank you again, Rhi, for all your help. It was decent of you to offer to come up here at such short notice to straighten out the paperwork. It really was loused up this time.'

'Pressure of work,' Rhiannon flicked a strand of glossy hair over her shoulder. 'I guess you should have a secretary permanently working with you on tour these days, instead of shuffling the mail backwards and forwards between the office in London and you on the move. There's sufficient work to keep a girl fully occupied.'

Eddie Beagle nodded emphatically. 'You're right—we must get extra staff. The bigger the success, the bigger the workload, but I'm not complaining.' He gave a broad smile. 'We'll all be millionaires in a year or two at this rate, and we'd rake in the cash even faster if only they'd agree to longer tours.' He turned to Rhiannon. 'Can't you persuade David?'

'I don't intend to try,' she retorted, the Welsh lilt in her voice emphasised by her flicker of annoyance. 'You're their manager, you do your own dirty work. All you think about is money!'

Eddie grinned his unabashed acknowledgment.

'In any case,' she continued earnestly, 'even if David could be persuaded, you'd still have Shane to deal with, and you know how he detests touring. He's told you he won't do any more, and he means it,' she warned. 'He's not as amenable as Brad was.'

'You still miss Brad, don't you?' The older man gave her a searching glance in the half light.

'Of course.' For an instant her composure slipped to expose a soft look of wistfulness. She bit her lip, then, with a brisk mental squaring of her shoulders, resumed the conversation. 'Don't insist on long tours,' she suggested. 'It's far better to pace the action and allow the group sufficient time to recover. You don't want the three of them to develop ulcers! They have little enough time for recuperation as it is. There's the new album to be compiled, and the big London concert, then the Far Eastern tour, not to mention television appearances and a million and one other things.' She wrinkled her nose. 'Give them a break! They've been on the road for nearly four weeks and played in fifteen different cities. You know how strenuous it is, and boring. Thank goodness the tour is nearly finished—one more date here, then up to Glasgow, then home.' She grinned at him. 'You're just greedy.'

'I know,' Eddie replied. 'But this is a dream come true. I've been waiting all my life for a success story like Submission's. I've managed other groups, but none have had the charisma, and brought in the cash, like this combination. If they work hard now I'll be able to retire a wealthy man. But you never know how long you'll be at the top in this business, the public are notoriously fickle, so that's why the effort must be now.' He punched a fist into the air in emphasis. 'They must grab all they can while their records are in the charts. Who can tell, in a couple of years' time they might not rate a mention. Some groups go on for ever, but others disappear overnight.' He glanced towards the stage. 'I do wish Shane would smile more.'

Rhiannon laughed at his frown of disapproval. 'Don't be silly—the girls love him because he's so arrogant. If he suddenly took it into his head to start smiling and winking at the audience he'd lose half his fans overnight. It's the mean, moody and magnificent image that thrills them, and, to be honest, he's never very relaxed on stage.'

'Or with the media, or with the fans,' Eddie added.

Rhiannon nodded her agreement. It was surprising that a good-looking man like Shane didn't accept the female admiration of his fans as his natural right. David and Tony, both attractive young men, positively expected to be drooled over and enjoyed every minute of the fuss, flirting and teasing the fans, but Shane shied away, always uneasy when surrounded by a crowd of wide-eyed admirers. She glanced at the chunky gold watch on her wrist. 'I'm going back to the hotel, before all hell is let loose at the end of the show.'

'I'll be along in half an hour,' Eddie told her. 'I want to hear the reception to that new instrumental. I think it's rather highbrow myself, but Shane insisted it be included.' He sighed. 'I'm worried about Shane. He's becoming more and more uptight as the tour progresses. The constant clamour of the fans and the press is getting on his nerves. He's like a volcano, ready to erupt. I just hope he manages to finish the tour without an explosion. I don't think he's really cut out for the pop world, do you?'

Rhiannon shrugged her shoulders. She agreed wholeheartedly with his statement, but knew her confirmation would merely depress him, and there seemed little point in worrying him unnecessarily; he was under enough pressure as it was, with the burgeoning success of the group, without added anxieties.

She left the theatre and walked briskly through the city streets to a large hotel only a short distance away. Its entire sixth floor had been reserved for Submission and their party, for when they toured a large entourage travelled with them—singers, back-up band, technicians responsible for the vast tonnage of musical equipment, amplifiers and lighting, a woman who cared for the stage clothes, and two full-time bodyguards. The bodyguards were the busiest people around, for wherever the group went they had to be protected from hordes of screaming fans, eager for autographs or wanting to embrace their idols. Eddie Beagle had travelled the route of the tour many months ago, and had long discussions with various hotel managements about security, until eventually, everyone was satisfied that the arrangements were foolproof. Only one lift would stop at the sixth floor while Submission were in residence at the Manchester hotel, and passes were required to board this lift. The stairways were constantly patrolled by security personnel employed by the hotel. Yet again Rhiannon showed her pass, this time to the lift attendant. He pressed the button for the sixth floor.

'Just come back from the theatre?' He was young, spotty and interested.

'Yes.'

'You're David Davies's sister, aren't you?' he enquired eagerly. 'You were going to marry Brad Holmes before he was killed in that motorbike accident.'

Instinctively Rhiannon lowered her head and clamped her full lips into a straight line. She resented complete strangers discussing her private life; it happened only rarely, but always distressed her.

'I'm sorry, I didn't mean to upset you.' The liftman had noticed her withdrawal.

'It's all right,' she assured him with a small smile. She suddenly felt weary. She had no wish to revive memories which still had the power to hurt.

'Shane Santiago is a terrific replacement, isn't he?' the liftman continued regardlessly.

'He's good.' The reply was flatly automatic.

'I'm a great fan of Submission,' he explained, warming to his subject, 'and you must admit that it's only since Shane Santiago has been with them that they've really hit the big time. Everything he writes is a winner, I reckon he's the reason for their success.'

Rhiannon straightened her shoulders. 'Don't forget Brad composed their first hit song,' she said defiantly, her dark eyes flashing. 'He was in at the beginning and his efforts played an important part in originally promoting the group. Shane came in as the momentum was picking up, so he hasn't been responsible for all their popularity.'

'Perhaps you're right,' the young man said politely, though it was perfectly clear from his tone that he didn't consider she was right at all, 'but Submission were very lucky that Shane took over when Brad was killed,' he insisted, refusing to leave the matter alone.

'I suppose so,' she said tiredly. It was a relief when the lift reached its destination and the conversation was terminated. She walked along the deserted corridor to her room, thankful to be alone. At the moment everything was quiet, but in an hour's time, when the show was over and everyone returned, the place would be buzzing. There was always an atmosphere of sparkling delight after a successful gig, when everyone relaxed and let off steam. The previous evening she had joined in the fun and friendly camaraderie, but tonight was different. She didn't want to laugh and talk, she wanted to be alone. She hung a 'Do Not Disturb' sign on the bedroom door and closed it firmly. Her room was in darkness, illuminated only by the glow from electric lamps in the city street below. She crossed to the window and looked up into the starless sky. She felt melancholy, for the music at the show and the conversation in the lift had provoked memories. Submission had come a long way in three years. Originally they had been a group of friends, all students at a London music school—Tony, Brad Holmes and her young brother, David. Rhiannon had worked as a secretary in the city, sharing a flat with another girl, and David had introduced her to Brad and Tony when he had come up from Wales to start his course. There had been instant, mutual attraction between her and Brad, and from then on she had spent most of her free time listening as they practised their music, and talking into the early hours about the possibility of forming a group. Shane, a friend of Tony's, had left music college several years previously, and was currently working with a Spanish symphony orchestra. He had collaborated lightheartedly with Brad on several songs, and on his brief visits to England, to see his mother, he always came round to hear the latest news and see how they were progressing. In the beginning Submission had played for college discos and at pubs, but within months their local popularity had soared and they were suddenly in great demand.

Rhiannon sighed in the darkness. Everything had been so good then. She and Brad had been deeply in love and their wedding had been arranged, then he had been killed, skidding on black ice one winter evening just a few weeks before they were due to be married. She nibbled nervously at the tip of a lacquered nail. If only she could turn the clock back! She closed the curtains and undressed. Although it was early she knew she would sleep. She yawned tiredly. The three days since she had joined the tour had been strenuous, as she had sought to make sense of the mass of paperwork which had built up over the past weeks. Now, thank goodness, everything was orderly again. She glanced across at the desk, for her bedroom had been turned into a makeshift office. The files were neatly stacked and she knew that a morning's hard work would clear most of the correspondence which demanded prompt action.

She was awake bright and early, and plunged beneath the shower before putting on a matching khaki-coloured blouse and skirt in heavy cotton. She twisted her hair back into a heavy knot at the nape of her neck and put only a whisper of pale green eyeshadow and a touch of mascara on her lashes before going for breakfast. Eddie was at the table in the private dining room, tucking in heartily to a plate of ham and eggs, when she appeared.

'Everyone's still in bed,' he said, reaching across to pour her a cup of coffee. 'How about us making an early start on today's post? Then you can tackle that batch of replies I dictated yesterday, and with luck you should be clear by lunchtime. Why don't you take a break this afternoon? You've been cooped up indoors ever since you arrived.'

Rhiannon smiled. 'That's a good idea, I'd love some fresh air.'

'I'll probably be tied up phoning London and the Far East for most of the morning, so if I'm not around just leave the letters on the desk and I'll sign them later.'

It was almost noon and Rhiannon was slipping the carbon paper out of the final letter when Shane walked into the room. He looked virile in a short-sleeved, red knit sports shirt and blue jeans. It was obvious he had just showered, for his long black hair curled damply over his collar.

'Nice to see someone doing something useful!' He folded his arms and raised a derisive brow. He studied her for a long moment, and then grinned suddenly, his teeth dazzling white in the sultriness of his face. 'I've been in bed most of the morning and I still feel lethargic.' He stretched lazily with the unconscious grace of a wild cat and strode past her to look out of the window, thumbs tucked into his broad leather belt. 'These tours are feast or famine,' he complained. 'It's either so bloody boring you think you'll fade away into the wallpaper, or else there's enough nervous energy being generated to split you into a thousand fragments.' He perched on the arm of the studded leather armchair alongside her desk and stretched out his long, muscular legs. 'There's no freedom. We're marooned in this damned hotel! And yet everyone imagines the entertainment world is pure unadulterated fun.' He shook his curly head in disgust, 'God! If they only knew. At least you've no illusions, Rhi, you're not deceived by the phoney glamour and image-making. And the things we have to do! That photo session yesterday really made me cringe—jolly smiles at the ready, shirts oh, so casually unbuttoned to reveal regulation gold medallions and manly chests——'

His blue eyes flashed angrily. 'I hate being a so-called sex symbol. What kind of a musician am I if people prefer to count the number of hairs on my chest rather than listen to the songs I write? It's degrading! I'm too old to be a teenager's delight.'

Rhiannon laughed at his grim expression. 'You're only thirty-three, Shane, that's hardly ancient. You could go on for years being a heart-throb.'

He rubbed a weary hand across his face and looked at her. 'I don't want to be a heart-throb, at least not a public one. And why is it that when every other woman appears to be falling over herself to get a glimpse of me, you won't even let me take you out to dinner?'

The reply was trite. 'I don't believe in mixing business and pleasure.' This was a matter they had been over many times in the past.

'Rubbish!'

'It's true.' Rhiannon looked at him levelly through steady brown eyes. 'If we developed some kind of . . .' she paused, 'attachment, it could make it difficult for us to work together in such close proximity. It could upset the harmony, and besides, I really do prefer to keep my private life entirely separate from work.'

He got to his feet and gazed down at her impatiently. 'You're talking utter nonsense and you know it. What about your relationship with Brad? You never worried about that interfering with this precious harmony.'

'That was different.' She avoided his look, busying herself with the sheets of paper and envelopes.

'What are you afraid of?' Shane taunted, reaching out and gripping her jaw in his hand, forcing her to meet the challenge in his glittering eyes. Rhiannon was thankful he could not hear the tremulous thud of her heart as she squirmed, unsuccessfully, to release herself.

'I'm not such an ogre,' he insisted. 'Come out with me.'

'Good idea.' They both started in surprise at the sound of a third voice. Shane reluctantly relinquished his grasp and moved away from her. Eddie had come into the room and had caught the tail end of the conversation. 'You two go out and grab some fresh air while you can. It's a glorious day.'

'I'm busy,' Rhiannon said firmly, hurriedly sorting out the carbon copies with exaggerated attentiveness. 'I'm sure Shane can find someone else to go with.'

'Don't be silly,' Eddie insisted. 'You've typed up all the urgent correspondence, anything else can wait. Besides, you're looking a bit pale, a touch of sunshine would do you a power of good. Off you go—that's an order!'

'I'll collect my jacket,' Shane told her with a smug wink of triumph, 'and I suppose I'd better take my sun specs as a disguise, to confuse any stray fan.'

'Leave by the back entrance,' Eddie instructed. 'I noticed a group of girls in the lobby just now.'

'Headed, inevitably, by the dreaded Betsy,' Shane moaned wearily. 'How I wish that girl would transfer her affections to someone else!'

'Why don't you go down and talk to her?' Rhiannon suggested. 'Perhaps that would satisfy her and she'd go away.'

'I doubt it,' Eddie intervened. 'By keeping your distance, Shane, there's always the chance she'll get fed up and follow some other guy instead. If you give any encouragement it could get even worse. I've heard of some girls who spend years drifting around on the fringe of pop groups, just happy to have the chance to see and talk to the members occasionally!'

'I don't know what to do,' Shane admitted, running his hand through his thick hair, 'but I just wish she'd give me a break. What a waste of a life, hanging around hotels and going to our concerts, night after night. At least *we* get paid for it!'

Rhiannon wound down the window of Shane's BMW and grinned as the wind blew through her hair, tossing it about her head like a veil of chestnut lace. It was warm and sunny, with the freshness of spring in the air, and her enjoyment at the outing quickly brushed away her misgivings at being out alone with him.

'No need for these, thank goodness,' he said with a grin, stowing his dark glasses under the dashboard.

'Where are we going?' Rhiannon asked, pushing her hair out of her eyes.'

'The Derbyshire hills—that should appeal to your Welsh blood! The scenery is wonderful, wild and untamed. It's a great place for a walk, no screaming fans, just green grass and purple heather and peace.'

'How do you know about it?'

'Manchester was another childhood stopover,' he said brusquely. 'Don't forget I'm the original travelling man.'

She looked at him out of the corner of her eye. She was filled with curiosity and wanted to ask more, but his eyes were firmly fixed on the road ahead, and his tone had indicated that he wouldn't welcome further questioning. Shane was notoriously evasive about his past, but she had gleaned from odd comments that his childhood had been unhappy.

When they reached the hills he parked the car alongside a wide reservoir, and together they climbed up and up a grassy slope until they reached the crest and the patch of shimmering water below them had dwindled into the distance. The hillside was deserted, apart from a few uninterested sheep munching stoically. Shane took off his jacket for Rhiannon to sit on, and stretched out beside her in the sunshine.

'I wish I had more time to do things like this,' he mused, chewing on a long strand of grass as he squinted up into a cloudless, deep blue sky.

'Like what?'

'Like lying on grassy hillsides alone with you.' His eyes dropped to hold hers steadfastly, sending a message which made her almost unbearably aware of the vibrant maleness of him, the tangled black hair blowing across his brow, his lean, muscular body. He reached out a hand to pull her down towards him, but she resisted. 'Don't spoil things, Shane,' she pleaded, experiencing an unreasonable surge of panic.

'I don't want to spoil things, I want to make them better.' He sat up briskly and rubbed at his jaw with hard fingers. 'Why do you persist in stifling our friendship? You've dated plenty of guys since Brad died, but you refuse to go out with me. Who don't you trust, Rhiannon,' he paused significantly and flung the word at her harshly, 'yourself?'

'I don't want to complicate my working life—both our lives,' she insisted, her eyes lowered evasively beneath a fringe of thick dark brown lashes.

'That's no kind of answer,' he retorted. 'God knows, you and Brad were close enough, but that never upset matters, and it wouldn't alter anything if you and I became . . . close friends.'

'You mean lovers, don't you?' she ground out, her face flushed. 'You're talking to the wrong girl, Shane—my name isn't Maxine!'

He shrugged and looked away into the distance, his face stern. 'Let's leave Maxine out of this, shall we? It's you I'm interested in.'

'I don't want a lover.' Her reply was fierce. 'And especially not you!'

'Why not? It's because I've taken over Brad's place in Submission isn't it?' he challenged furiously, his face darkening with anger. 'And now you're afraid I'd be successful in taking his place in your life too—then you'd be forced to let go of his memory. It's bloody ironical,' he caught hold of her shoulder, twisting her body towards him. 'You'd have liked it better if the group had only had a lukewarm success with my music, then Brad's memory would have stayed shiny bright, and I would have been only second best. But I'm not, and I have no intention of being second best with you either.'

'God, you're arrogant! What makes you imagine you could ever mean anything to me?' she cried, glaring at him.

'Think it through, Rhiannon,' he growled, his dark Filipino ancestry emphasised in his rage, 'but don't imagine it makes any difference to my feelings. I want you, and I shall have you, make no mistake about that.' The look on his face was that of a predator, and Rhiannon's throat constricted with some emotion she could not name.

'Come on.' He held out a hand and pulled her roughly to her feet, then with long, impatient strides, he led the way down the hillside.

They sat in cold silence during the journey back to the city, each deliberately ignoring the other, but each stiffly aware of every tiny movement the other made.

'Back to civilisation,' Shane remarked sarcastically as he pulled the car to a halt at the rear of the hotel. He reached forward to retrieve his sunglasses. 'I suppose I'd better put these on until we're back in the safety of the sixth floor.' He gave her a rueful smile, and suddenly the mood changed, and the anger of their confrontation evaporated. 'How pleasant it would be if I didn't have to deal with all the publicity and the fans and the razzamatazz. My life has been moving in the wrong direction for quite a while. I must get off the merry-go-round, Rhi, before it's too late.' He stared out of the windscreen and gripped the steering wheel so tightly that the blood drained from his knuckles. 'I want to compose music *I* like and not necessarily what Eddie considers is marketable. I want to be me, not just a contrived package— Shane Santiago, pop star.'

'But you've been pleased with some of the records you've produced,' Rhiannon stressed quietly. 'You were delighted when they reached number one, and you enjoy having all the money they've earned. In a year or two when the heat is off you'll be able to indulge yourself and do whatever you wish. You'll be able to spend the rest of your life composing without any financial worries. Good heavens, most people would be ecstatic to possess a bank balance like yours!'

'You're right,' Shane sighed reluctantly. 'Perhaps I'm being unreasonable, but I feel so goddamn unsettled. All my life I've travelled around and now I feel the urge to stop being a wanderer, though it's a difficult habit to break. There's nothing permanent in my life, I'm like a mouse on a wheel, running like mad and getting precisely nowhere. However, no doubt I'll work something out.' He gave her a quick smile of mock despair, and climbed from the car. 'Are you coming to the theatre again this evening?'

She pushed back a wayward strand of hair from her brow and looked across at him over the top of the car. 'No. To be frank, one pop concert lasts me a long time.'

'Likewise,' Shane said tersely as he followed her into the hotel.

It was early evening when the sixth floor became quiet again. Most of the entourage had departed for the theatre and Rhiannon decided to complete the final batch of non-urgent letters. Dinner was always served late, after the show, and she would have at least three hours without interruption to clear the correspondence. She sat at her typewriter and chewed her lip, her mind hurtling back to Shane's furious accusation of the afternoon. How supremely confident he was, she thought irritably, to imagine he could ever take Brad's place in her affections. It was typical of his male self-assurance that it had never occurred to him that one reason for her keeping her distance might simply be that she didn't like him. But that wasn't true, she admitted reluctantly to herself, as she slipped a sheet of paper into the typewriter. Shane was a brutally handsome man, articulate and witty, and she was certainly not immune to his charms, but she knew she must resist. She owed it to

Brad. She would never allow Shane to eclipse his memory. It was enough that he had filled Brad's place in Submission, filled it so ably, but now he seemed to take it for granted that she would be his as well. Well, he was wrong! She was not part of some package deal, some perk that went with the job. She hit at the typewriter keys with unaccustomed severity—she was damned if she would become involved with him!

CHAPTER TWO

RHIANNON finished typing the letters and stacked them carefully away in a folder for Eddie's signature the following morning, then took out her check list and studied it carefully—she must remind Eddie about plane reservations for the Far Eastern tour and check whether visas were required for any of the countries. She rubbed a weary hand across her brow and scribbled furiously, then a series of rapid knocks at the bedroom door broke her concentration. Eddie looked past her at the folders on the desk, 'You're not still working, are you? For heaven's sake, pack it in for the night and come and have a drink with me while we wait for the others to return.'

Hastily she cleared away the papers and snapped off the light, following Eddie along the thickly carpeted hallway to a private lounge. The spacious room served as a meeting point for Submission and their employees and usually hummed with conversation and laughter, but just now it was empty. A well-known interior decorator was responsible for its ultra-modern appearance, with banks of stark black and white leather settees on a citrus yellow carpet. Abstract paintings in bright primary colours hung on the walls, and low glass and chrome tables carried copies of the latest glossy magazines.

'What'll you have?' Eddie asked, walking to a white leather-covered bar which filled one corner of the room.

'Campari soda, please.'

Rhiannon picked up a fashion magazine and began to leaf idly through it. She had changed earlier into a copper-coloured crêpe-de-chine blouse which she had teamed with dark brown hopsack pants, and the soft glow from the concealed lighting accentuated the subtle gleam of the material as she moved. She had brushed her hair, and now it fell loosely about her shoulders. She smiled up at Eddie as he handed her the glass.

'Marvellous, isn't it?' he grinned, and she knew from experience that he wasn't speaking of the tankard of beer in his hand. Eddie was incapable of accepting that the success he had waited for all his life was now actually his, and delighted in reminiscing about the humble beginnings of the group, which became even more humble each time he repeated the tale.

'It's difficult to believe that three years ago the lads were playing at college hops and in seedy bars,' he said with a satisfied smack of the lips, 'and that you organised their gigs for them when you'd finished work.'

Rhiannon sipped her drink and listened patiently. She knew the tale backwards, but had no wish to spoil Eddie's self-indulgent monologue.

'Then I heard about them, groomed them, made the important contacts. The recording company needed a bit of pushing before they'd risk that first record. It was a good thing I took over the reins from you,' he smiled. 'I don't reckon you'd have been hard enough to fight for the best for the lads. You have to be cut-throat in this game.' She nodded her agreement. It was true that she had disliked the management side, and had been relieved when Eddie appeared on the scene. He certainly had no compunction about arguing, fighting and wheedling to force better terms out of the recording companies, theatres and the many business interests who wanted a slice of Submission's earning power.

'I remember the very first fan letter,' Rhiannon reflected happily. 'David asked me to type a reply. I had no idea then that I'd end up running an office with three full-time secretaries.'

'Life has changed,' Eddie commented with a smug smile.

'It certainly has!'

'Off to Glasgow in the morning.'

'Thank goodness!' Rhiannon ran her finger around

the rim of her glass and sighed. 'And then the end. Everyone's ready for a rest.'

'Especially Shane.'

'He's getting edgier by the minute,' she agreed. 'I'm always amazed—the more the fans love him, the more he hates it, and the more he hates it, the more they love him.'

'He should learn to relax,' Eddie said impatiently, taking a gulp of beer and wiping his mouth with the back of his hand. 'He's too damned restless for his own good. He ought to settle down and enjoy life. He's young, he's healthy, he's famous, so what's the problem?'

'It's not as simple as that.'

Eddie gave a snort of disgust. 'Submission's been good to him. It's brought wealth, a world-wide audience for his music, and a whole host of admirers. Look at those hot romances he's indulged in with actresses and models, including Maxine, all because he's a member of the famous Submission.'

'Nonsense!' Rhiannon said tartly. 'With his looks he'd attract a crowd of willing women even if he was a filing clerk.'

'Not Maxine,' came the firm reply. 'She only sidled up to him when she realised Submission were heading for the top. She reckons she loves him, but she also loves the glamour and the publicity, his fancy car, being photographed at "in" parties with "in" people. She wouldn't give him a second glance if he wasn't famous.'

Rhiannon didn't agree with his last remark, but she let it pass.

'I wonder how she's enjoying modelling in the States?'

'She'll be having a whale of a time,' sneered Eddie. 'Swaying up and down Fifth Avenue in her ridiculous clothes and being escorted by ardent admirers to way-out discos and night clubs. No doubt she's working her way through a list of eligible, and not so eligible, millionaires!'

'She's not as bad as that,' Rhiannon protested with a laugh.

'She's a gold-digger, she rubs me up the wrong way. I can't imagine what Shane sees in her.'

'She is rather gorgeous,' Rhiannon pointed out, 'with that curtain of silvery blonde hair and pouty lips. She's in great demand as a model—look,' she riffled through the magazines and pulled one out, 'she's featured in here, doesn't she look fantastic?' She held out the photograph for Eddie to see.

'Humph! I don't know why you and Shane don't pair up. You'd be far better for him than Maxine.'

Rhiannon swirled the pink liquid in her glass and watched it silently, her lips compressed into a thoughtful line. So Eddie also imagined it was an unwritten law that she and Shane should be together. Well, she refused to conform. Just because she'd been in love with the leader of Submission once it didn't mean she would be again.

'I wonder if Maxine's had time to send Shane a postcard?' Eddie said contemptuously. 'I bet she's been too busy smiling for the cameras or swinging her hips in discos.' He stretched his arms above his head and yawned. 'One thing is certain, she wouldn't sit patiently waiting in some boring hotel.' He looked across at Rhiannon. 'Hey, I've just had a good idea. Why don't you come with us on the Far East tour? You said yourself we need a secretary, and it would give you a break. It'll be more relaxed, like a holiday,' he coaxed, 'and you'll get the chance to visit all those far away places—Malaysia, Singapore, Thailand. Go on, say you'll come!'

'I don't know,' Rhiannon tugged at her bottom lip with her teeth. 'Perhaps I will—can I decide later?'

'No rush. David was pleased you joined us this time and could meet his new girl-friend. Cheryl's a pretty little thing, isn't she? She and Kim make an attractive duo on stage and they harmonise well together. David seems very serious about her, although she's only been with us a few months.'

Rhiannon finished her drink and placed the glass on a side table.

'She's a nice girl,' she agreed. 'I think she'd be good for him, he needs someone with their feet on the ground. David tends to get carried away, but Cheryl realises how unpredictable show business can be. He imagines the glory will last for ever, he's turning into an applause freak.' She thought fondly of her brother. Although, at twenty-three, David was only two years her junior, his lack of responsibility and immature outlook made her feel positively ancient by comparison.

'Your parents must be very proud of him, he's done exceptionally well for such a young fellow.'

'Yes, they always watch him on television, and my mother bores her neighbours silly with tales of how marvellous he is! Mind you, she's always doted on him, and he twists her around his little finger. He's had a charmed life really, Mum's always protected him and indulged him. He started at the music school just after Dad had been forced to give up work through ill health, and it really was a struggle for them to afford to send him, but Mum insisted he should go, even though it meant they had to make drastic economies.'

'He's able to make it up to them now, though. Are they pleased with the house he's bought them?'

'They're delighted,' she grinned, 'It's on the edge of the village where they've spent all their married life. They always admired the house, but never in their wildest dreams did they imagine they would ever live there. It's beautiful. David heard, purely by chance, that it was for sale, and he went across to South Wales and bought it for them. He's very generous. They're in the seventh heaven. Dad's health has improved dramatically, and I'm sure it's because he doesn't have money worries any more. David has promised to look after them financially.'

There was a babble of voices in the corridor, and the

door burst open. The show had finished and everyone was returning.

'Hi, Rhi—Eddie.' David walked across to them, grinning broadly as he peeled off his white jacket. 'Tonight's performance was another ace, we went down great!' He flopped down beside Rhiannon as members of the back-up band filtered into the room and made their way to the bar for a quick drink before supper. Some waved a friendly greeting as they passed by, while others stopped for a brief word.

'We had to do three encores,' David continued happily, tugging at a lock of his blond hair. 'The audience refused to let us go. You should have heard the noise!—I thought the roof was going to lift off with all the foot-stamping and cheers.'

'It was a good show,' Eddie agreed. 'It was going well when I left.'

'Time to get changed.' David began to undo the silver buttons of his waistcoat. 'Tony and Shane have already gone to their rooms. I'll collect Cheryl, she's struggling out of those foxy tight pants of hers, and then we can all have dinner. I'm starving!'

'Another drink, Rhi?' Eddie asked when David had departed.

'No, thanks, I'll wait until we eat, then I'll have some wine.'

Eddie went over to the bar and poured himself another beer. The room was noisy. Rhiannon chatted, listening to the enthusiastic reports on the evening's show. Everyone was in a good mood, drunk on success, and she decided that perhaps touring wasn't so bad after all.

'Do you have the map giving the Glasgow route?' Eddie asked, taking a mouthful of beer.

She nodded. 'It's straightforward. We take the motorway as far as the border, then the A74. Shall I drive your Ford Granada again?'

'If you would, please. It gives me a chance to rest. Shane will be driving his car. Perhaps a good burn up along the motorway will clear his frustrations. Could you get the map for me now? I'd feel happier if I had the route sorted out in my mind.'

'Sure.'

She left the crowded lounge and walked down the hallway towards her bedroom. Suddenly there was an angry shout from the end of the corridor and a door was flung open violently. There was more shouting and the sound of an indignant reply. Rhiannon recognised Shane's voice and started to run towards his room.

'Get out!' he was bellowing. 'Get the hell out of here!' Her heart sank. He sounded furious. The strength of his anger was frightening, but she knew she must intervene and try to deflect an ugly scene. As she approached he stood in the doorway to his room, stripped to the waist, glaring savagely at someone Rhiannon could not see.

'Leave me alone!' he snarled, quivering with rage. 'Don't you think I'm entitled to some privacy? How dare you come in here!'

'What's the matter?' Rhiannon asked breathlessly as she reached him, and he turned to glower at her, enveloping her in his anger. His nostrils flared and he looked very dark and foreign, the chiselled planes of his face tense and forbidding. His fists were clenched at his sides. 'That bloody girl!' he growled belligerently. 'If she doesn't leave me alone I'll go mad!'

Rhiannon tried, unsuccessfully, to ignore his black rage as she pushed past him into the room. He stepped smartly in beside her, slamming shut the door, and she could hear him at her shoulder, breathing erratically as he struggled to control the fury within him. Betsy stood at the end of the bed, sullenly twisting a handkerchief in her fingers.

'What's happened?' asked Rhiannon. 'What are you doing here?'

'I came to see you, Shane.' Betsy raised her plump chin in defiance and spoke directly to him, ignoring Rhiannon. 'I love you.'

Shane made an impatient sound at the back of his throat. 'You follow me around incessantly,' he groaned, his muscular chest rising and falling rapidly. 'You saw me on stage this evening, wasn't that enough? You're suffocating me, and wasting your time. For heaven's sake go away and do something useful. In any case how did you manage to get into my room?' He rounded on Rhiannon angrily. 'Why were the security guards so slack? No outsiders are allowed up here—I understood Eddie had it all arranged?'

She flinched and took a step back, momentarily stunned by the fury in his voice.

'It's all my fault,' Betsy answered. 'I waited until one of the guards was answering the telephone, and then I ran up the stairs.'

'And hid in my bathroom,' Shane accused. 'I could have walked in there stark naked!'

For an instant Rhiannon had a foolish urge to laugh, he sounded so puritanical and outraged. She gave a smothered giggle, but he flashed her a glance so furious that it promptly wiped away her humour.

'What a scandal that could have caused!' he continued bitterly. 'I can imagine the headlines—"Pop Star Accused of Seducing Teenager", when nothing could be farther from the truth. I'm much too old for a schoolgirl like you.'

'I'm not a schoolgirl,' Betsy protested vehemently, 'I'm eighteen and I work in a factory. When I've earned enough money I pack it in and follow Submission around. I've seen all your concerts,' she added, two indignant spots of bright colour on her cheeks.

'What about your other interests?' Shane asked with a heavy sigh. 'A boy-friend, some hobbies?'

'I only live for you,' declared Betsy.

'Oh God!' he muttered, rubbing the back of his neck with long fingers. Rhiannon was relieved to see that his anger was beginning to subside.

'I have all your records,' continued Betsy proudly, 'and I collect magazines and posters. My bedroom walls are covered with pictures of you, Shane. I spend all my money on Submission.'

He sank down on the bed. 'That's stupid,' he shook

his head in disbelief. 'Surely you realise David, Tony and I are just ordinary people? Don't turn us into gods. You mustn't believe all the trash you read, honestly we're just the same as everyone else.'

'You're not.'

'I am.' His eyes hardened with a flicker of anger, and Rhiannon held her breath. Please let him keep cool, she implored silently, watching a nerve twitch at the corner of his eye.

'I am,' Shane insisted again, then his tone softened, and Rhiannon let out a breath in relief. 'I'm just the same as anyone's brother, or boy-friend. I like the things you like—picnics, swimming, a good book, listening to music. I'm not a member of the jet set, in fact I'm incredibly dull.'

'I don't believe you.' Betsy remembered the information she had gleaned from magazine articles. 'You're special. You're an international gipsy, I read it in a newspaper. You have lots of girl-friends, all glamorous and sexy, and you're always changing them, and you like fast cars and discos. I know all about you,' she announced triumphantly, daring him to deny the evidence she had collected.

'That was in the past and exaggerated beyond recognition,' Shane raked his fingers through his jet black curls. 'It's an image the journalists create. Okay, so I drive a powerful car and I go to an occasional disco, but I also enjoy quieter pastimes. The entertainment world has some attractions, but they soon pall. It's an artificial life. I'm thirty-three years old, and I want to settle down and compose some really worthwhile music. As far as girl-friends are concerned,' he continued, 'I have just one—a steady one. Rhiannon here is my girl-friend.' He stood up and pulled Rhiannon close to him, looking down at her, cautiously narrowing his blue eyes as if daring her to resist. She was well aware he was play-acting for Betsy's benefit, but the sudden closeness of his half naked body disturbed her.

'Put your arms around my neck, darling,' he said,

tightening his grasp, 'show Betsy how much you love me, then she'll realise I'm telling the truth.' The look in his eyes was compelling. Slowly Rhiannon reached up and put her arms around his neck, and Shane bent his head and kissed her. At first she remained carefully impassive, aware she was participating in a charade, nothing more, but then his kiss changed. His mouth became hard and insistent, forcing her lips apart, until she felt herself drowning helplessly in the heady thrill of his embrace. His strong hands moved on her back, holding her closer and closer until she felt the hardness of the full stretch of his body against hers. He pushed his fingers into her tumble of chestnut hair and his breathing quickened. It seemed as though their hearts were beating in unison.

'Oh!' Betsy gasped from across the room. The spell was broken. Rhiannon struggled from his grasp, her brown eyes wide and startled, her pulses racing, and touched her bruised lips softly with the back of her hand.

'I think that proves there's good chemistry between us, don't you, Rhi?' Shane grinned, arrogantly raising one superior black brow. Rhiannon snapped back to life and glared at him.

'Now then, darling,' he said, a mischievous glitter dancing in his eyes, 'don't forget we have an audience. You mustn't get carried away and make love to me with Betsy here, even though I know you want to.'

Rhiannon blushed furiously. Damn him, he'd known all along exactly what he was doing! He had trapped her, forced her to respond, and was now enjoying the knowledge of that response. How she wished she had been able to remain calm and cool beneath his touch, but he had sent the blood pounding through her veins as Brad used to, driving away any semblance of reason.

'I'll go,' Betsy piped up. 'I didn't know you had a girl-friend—a serious girl-friend, I mean. When are you going to get married?' Love and marriage were tangled inextricably in Betsy's romantic mind. One meant the other.

'Not for a long time,' Rhiannon said quickly, trying to put some space between her and Shane, but he stopped her, holding her tight against his chest. She noticed, irrationally, how the dark hair formed a cross at his breastbone, and that a thick hairy vertical line disappeared downwards across the flat plane of his stomach. His skin was pale gold, a legacy from his Filipino blood.

'Take no notice,' Shane grinned. 'She wouldn't give you the date even if she knew it, but believe me, it will be soon.'

Rhiannon shot him a furious look and dug her fingernails into the wrist that was holding her.

'You little . . .!' he snatched his arm away and rubbed it ruefully. Betsy paid no attention, she was engrossed in her own thoughts.

'I won't trouble you again,' she said, pulling distractedly at her grey sweater, 'now that I know you're going to be married.' She bent her head and walked dejectedly towards the door. Shane put his hands on her arms to stop her, and planted a brief kiss on her brow. The girl gazed up at him, thunderstruck. Then she turned and went out, closing the door softly behind her.

'You bastard!' Rhiannon spat out. Shane smiled with masculine delight.

'Me? What have I done? There was no reason to attack me.' He rubbed his wrist again.

Rhiannon spluttered, anger making her momentarily speechless.

'What have you done!' she managed to say at last. 'You told her I was your girl-friend and that we were going to be married. If some reporter picks that up it'll be in all the newspapers, and we'll both be followed around by the media for weeks. And you treated both Betsy and me with contempt, you. . . .' She was lost for words, then, 'You male chauvinist pig!' she accused violently.

He laughed, tossing back his head. 'Now then, Rhi,

don't allow that Celtic blood of yours to make you melodramatic. I merely wanted to get rid of Betsy, and I appear to have succeeded.'

'And then you go and kiss her in such a pitifully condescending way,' Rhiannon stormed. 'The poor girl probably won't wash for weeks, she'll be showing the spot to all her friends—"Look, here's where Shane Santiago kissed me",' she mimicked ruthlessly.

'I guess you're right,' he had the grace to look shamefaced, 'I was overdoing it, but I wasn't being condescending when I kissed you.' He reached out and took hold of her arm. 'You turn me on. Kiss me again.'

'No!' She fought to free herself from his grasp.

'Okay, okay,' he grinned, releasing her, 'don't attack me again, you have sharp nails. I see I'm not the only one around here with a hot temper. I'll leave you alone. Wait until I'm changed and then we'll join the others for dinner, they'll be wondering where we've got to.'

He grabbed a pair of jeans and a tee-shirt from the bed and swung nonchalantly into the bathroom. Rhiannon breathed heavily. She was relieved that he did not appear to have realised just how much he had aroused her. Her body had never felt so tender to the touch. She rubbed her forehead wearily and gradually the throbbing pulses slackened.

'That could be the answer to all my problems,' Shane said through the half open door. 'If I were married perhaps the fans would leave me alone, and I'd feel more settled.'

'You'd better propose to Maxine, then,' she answered tartly, sitting on the bed and trying to tame her tousled hair with her fingers.

'Marry Maxine? You must be joking! She's definitely not the settling down type. Can you imagine her in a house in the country with a brood of kids?' He peered round the door, rapidly brushing his thick, glossy hair. Rhiannon allowed herself a small smile. The image of Maxine with her way-out clothes and immaculate make-up plodding around ploughed fields and lanes did appear ridiculous.

'Besides,' Shane continued, returning to the bedroom fully dressed, 'we've virtually packed it in. It was a very shortlived affair. She left for the States with no strings attached to either of us. A little bit of Maxine goes a long way. She's too frantic, always wanting to show herself off at first nights, or the latest night club.' His voice became serious. 'You're not like that, are you?'

'I am,' Rhiannon told him defiantly, determined not to fit into the mould he wanted to make for her. 'I love dining out and dancing.'

'But not obsessively, not every night?'

'No,' she was forced to admit.

He sat down on the bed beside her. 'I'm considering leaving the group, Rhi.' Her heart stood still. She'd half expected this decision for a long time, it was inevitable, and yet his words still came as a shock. His departure would bring chaos.

'I'm basically a composer, that's what I'm best at. I feel uneasy appearing on stage. It was different when I was with the orchestra, I was anonymous then.'

Rhiannon gave an inward smile at his modest lack of insight. She was positive many a female classical music fanatic had singled out the handsome pianist and searched rapidly through the programme for his name.

'Now I only have to raise an eyebrow, or swing my damn pelvis, and the screams multiply,' he continued bitterly. 'If we played "Auld Lang Syne" all evening we would still achieve an identical ecstatic reaction. It wouldn't be so bad if we just made records and didn't have to do the shows.'

Rhiannon opened her mouth to protest, but he raised a firm hand to silence her.

'I know what you're going to say, that I can't have one side of success without the other, and you're probably right.' He rubbed his jaw worriedly. 'But it's not only being on stage that's the problem, though that's bad enough—no one reacts naturally to me anymore. They aren't interested in the real me, they only want the image—the superficial pop star. It's wearing me down, I feel I don't know who I am any more. Look at tonight,' he complained, waving a dismissive hand, 'that silly girl Betsy, spending all her time following us around. She has no notion of what we're really like as people, she's only interested in a cardboard creation.'

'You can't break up the group,' Rhiannon protested. 'What about David and Tony, and Eddie? He's waited all his life for a success like Submission's—you can't snatch that away from him.'

'I must change things,' Shane replied, his gaze direct and forceful from beneath his dark lashes.

'Don't do anything rash. Leaving the group is a very big step. Think it over carefully, consider the others.'

'Do you imagine I don't lie awake at night worrying myself sick about the consequences?' he asked tersely. 'Believe me, I have no wish to let anyone down, but it's vital I take control of my own destiny. I originally agreed to join Submission on a temporary basis while Brad was in hospital after his crash, but then the records were hits and suddenly we were famous. I certainly never anticipated that!' He shook his head wearily. 'Eddie knows how I feel, but he keeps jollying me along. I'm waiting for the popularity to fade, Rhi, but at the rate we're going I don't think it will, at least not for two or three years, and I can't hang on that long.' His next three words were like shots from a pistol. *I want out.*'

'It's not that bad,' Rhiannon coaxed.

Shane gave a short, humourless laugh. 'I thought at least you'd understand.'

'I do, Shane, but you can't just quit.'

'What do I do, then? Close my eyes and think of England?' he grimaced. 'We shall be on the move for several months this year, and I had enough travelling when I was a kid to last me a lifetime. I need some stability.' He looked at her for a long moment, then, 'I like you,' he said, his blue eyes darkening with emotion.

'I like you, too,' she replied lightly, endeavouring to break the highly charged atmosphere which was threatening to pull them inexorably together.

He reached out and took her hand. 'You could help me sort myself out.'

Rhiannon stood up, avoiding the unspoken significance of his words. She shook back her hair. 'We'd better go and get something to eat,' she suggested, 'the others will be waiting.'

'Where have you two been?' Eddie queried as they entered the dining room. The round table was set for seven, and five of the places were already taken. The back-up band and other members of the entourage ate in the hotel coffee shop, but for the sake of security Submission with the two girl singers, Eddie and Rhiannon, ate their meals in a private room on the sixth floor. A waiter hovered impatiently in the background, a covered tureen of soup at his elbow, and Rhiannon sat down hastily.

'The dreaded Betsy invaded my room,' Shane explained as he joined her at the table. There was a murmur of concern.

'How did that happen? The security arrangements were supposed to be foolproof. I hope there weren't any fireworks?' Eddie asked anxiously.

'Don't worry,' Shane shot a sidelong glance at Rhiannon, 'I sent her off happily with a goodbye kiss. It's amazing how contented women become when you kiss them!'

Rhiannon shook out a stiff white napkin across her lap, studiously ignoring the teasing sexual undercurrent in his voice. As the waiter served the soup she was disturbingly aware of Shane beside her, his hard, muscular thigh against hers. Until he had kissed her she had been able to successfully ignore his unconscious sensuality, but now she remembered the tantalising feel of his mouth on hers, and felt herself grow pink. She concentrated on buttering a dinner roll as she tried desperately to eliminate her heightened awareness of his closeness. As if sensing her thoughts Shane glanced sideways at her and grinned. Their eyes caught and held.

'I'm ready for this,' Eddie lifted his spoon. 'By the way, I thought the reaction to your new number was a trifle tepid, Shane, didn't you?'

With an effort Shane tore his eyes from Rhiannon.

'Yes, I did. To be frank, the number would go down better with a more discerning audience. After all, give teenagers a heavy beat and a loud guitar and they're happy.'

'That's not true!' David broke in. 'Plenty of them enjoy more serious music.'

'Not our lot,' retorted Shane heatedly.

'Let's face it, Shane,' Tony intervened, 'you've always wanted to write something more upmarket, a modern opera, for example.'

Shane nodded his dark head emphatically. 'Yes, I have, and I'm damn well going to do it, too, in the near future. I've had enough of this present set-up, with the constant fans and the media.'

Everyone turned their heads at the latent threat in his voice. Rhiannon felt a flinty fear grip the pit of her stomach.

'In fact,' he announced calmly, looking at her directly with piercing blue eyes, 'the only way I'd be prepared to stay on with Submission is if Rhiannon agrees to marry me.'

CHAPTER THREE

'No, I will *not*!' Rhiannon said sharply, grinding into first gear with an unusual display of ill temper, 'I will *not* marry Shane!' Her face was pale. A sleepless night, twisting irritably between the sheets, had left mauve smudges beneath her eyes and a headache throbbed dully in her left temple as she swung the steering wheel of the big car and pulled jaggedly from the forecourt of the hotel out into the city traffic. Eddie sat beside her, the map on his knee, and Tony and Kim were settled comfortably in the rear seats. Eddie swivelled to look out of the back window.

'Good, Shane's right behind. He'll follow until we hit the motorway and then he'll be off, he knows the route from there.'

Moving Submission, the equipment and the employees was a major undertaking. A huge pantechnicon, carrying tons of amplifiers, instruments and stage gear, had departed at the crack of dawn on its long slow journey north. After an early breakfast the band and technicians had driven off in a minibus, and now the three members of the group, the girl singers, Eddie and Rhiannon, were to follow in two cars. Rhiannon kept an eye open for the directions to the M6 motorway and soon the busy city centre was left behind.

'You like Shane,' Eddie insisted, returning again to the subject uppermost in his mind, 'he's young, good-looking and wealthy—what more do you want?'

'I want love,' the words were snapped out staccato fashion, 'I don't want an arranged marriage. I refuse to allow Shane to make up my mind for me. This isn't the eighteenth century, and I won't be told whom I should marry. It's preposterous!'

'But you'd be ideal for each other,' Eddie's voice was

calm and reasonable. 'You're fully conversant with the strains and stresses he's under, you'd be able to make him relax.'

Rhiannon gritted her teeth.

'It would be the same life style as if you'd married Brad,' Kim's remark floated over from the back seat.

'It would *not*,' Rhiannon bit out angrily, glaring at the pixie faced girl through the driving mirror. 'Brad wasn't as intense as Shane. He enjoyed being in Submission, he would never have treated me like this.'

'But you like Shane,' Eddie repeated.

'Yes, I like him,' she acknowledged grimly, accelerating with a touch of recklessness as a clear stretch of road appeared ahead, 'but that's not sufficient reason to marry him.' Her hands curled tightly around the steering wheel in frustration as she remembered Shane's words on the grassy hillside—'I want you, and I shall have you—make no mistake about that.' Now it seemed as though he was carrying through his threat, but surely he didn't expect her to submit to his will? Her brown eyes sparked with temper. There was no way she would agree to his ridiculous idea.

Tony leaned forward, his untidy fair hair falling into his eyes, 'He's very fond of you, he's always fancied you.'

'My landlord fancies me, and the bass player in the band,' Rhiannon retorted tartly, struggling to keep her patience, 'but I have absolutely no intention of marrying them either. It's one thing to fall in love naturally, as Brad and I did, and build up a relationship which leads to marriage, but it's an entirely different matter to be used as a pawn in a game, merely to keep everyone happy.'

'Shane's very sexy,' Kim chirped.

'You marry him, then!'

'But Rhi, he wants *you*,' Eddie intervened. 'After you stormed out of the dining room last night we had a long discussion.'

'Behind my back!' The Welsh accent was strong.

'It had to be behind your back. You refused to listen, if you remember, and disappeared to your room in a huff.'

Rhiannon shrugged, and as she turned off on to the slip road for the motorway there was a glimpse of the sleek BMW 735 as it swung out smoothly to overtake. She glanced sideways and for a split second her eye caught Shane's as he drew alongside. He grinned mischievously, raising his fingers in a quick salute, then pulled powerfully ahead, until the silver car was embroiled in the fast-moving lanes of traffic. Damn him! she thought furiously. He would be well aware of the fraught conversation which was taking place, and was obviously amused. She had taken her breakfast in her room that morning to avoid him and his outrageous proposition, for she had no wish to become further tangled up in his scheming.

'If Shane deserts us now the whole thing would fall to pieces,' Eddie persevered, ignoring the look of wild exasperation on her face. 'The money would dry up virtually overnight. His presence is essential—musicians like him don't grow on trees.'

'We'd never find anyone as good as Shane, he's the catalyst that made us successful,' Tony inserted quickly. 'He has the perfect image. His dark looks make a great contrast with David and me, *and* he's a brilliant keyboard player. Without him Submission would go downhill—fast!'

'Nonsense!' her tone was crisp. 'He'd probably be prepared to continue writing and arranging the songs, so the records would still be the same. You'd only be without him on stage, there must be plenty of guys who could fill the gap. And *he* didn't make you successful, you had a hit song when Brad was alive,' she pointed out frostily.

'We haven't forgotten that,' Eddie agreed quietly as he reached into his jacket pocket for cigarettes, 'But Shane *has* written and performed all the subsequent chart toppers and despite what he feels personally about appearing on stage, his public image is good. He has a tremendous following of his own.'

The bulk of the traffic on the wide motorway was beginning to disperse, turning off to the various industrial centres of Lancashire, and now the road was clearer. Rhiannon settled herself back in the upholstered seat for the four-hour journey. The BMW had disappeared from sight, for Shane was a fast and skilful driver.

'A new musician would need months of training,' Tony said earnestly. 'He'd have to learn to play our numbers in our style, and do the routines. There's a hell of a lot of work involved, *and* he'd have to be acceptable to the fans—it would be difficult to find someone who fitted in so well with David and me.'

'Shane slotted in easily enough as a replacement for Brad,' she pointed out with a tiny twinge of conscience. If she was honest Shane had not only replaced Brad, he had far outshone him.

'That was different.'

'No, it wasn't.'

'Shane came in near the beginning when there wasn't so much at stake.' Eddie lit his cigarette and tossed the spent match from the car window. 'I suppose we could find a replacement if we really had to, though it would take a good twelve months to achieve a smooth takeover. We could introduce someone gradually into the group, begin to phase out Shane, and keep our fingers tightly crossed that the new combination would be as successful as the old one.'

'Why don't you marry Shane for a year?' Kim asked from the back seat. 'Have some kind of contract, then get a divorce. It would keep him happy and give Submission time to find a new guy.'

Rhiannon snorted in disgust.

'Why not?' Eddie inhaled deeply. 'That's a great idea. Of course, the press and public would never know anything about it. You could have a business contract—I'd draw it up for you. All you would have to do would be pretend to be in love, just create a façade. It could all be purely platonic, if that's what you want.'

'I don't think that's what Shane has in mind,' Tony remarked with a wide grin.

'You'd have to be out of your tiny mind to want a platonic relationship,' Kim sniggered. Rhiannon clenched her teeth, holding back a suitably sarcastic retort.

'Let's look at this thing calmly and coolly,' suggested Eddie, 'purely from a business viewpoint, okay?'

Rhiannon sighed crossly, but nodded her head. It was obvious she would be given no peace until they had talked the matter through. Eddie held up one finger. 'Firstly, Shane was saying last night that he needs some kind of protection from the fans, and it's obvious that news of his marriage, plus the usual interviews and lovey-dovey newlywed pictures in the press would take the heat out of the situation. Secondly,' he raised another finger, 'if Shane leaves straight away, which he's threatening to do, the success of Submission could fade drastically, which would be disastrous for Tony, David and me. There's a hefty chunk of tax to be paid, and a mass of outgoings to be dealt with. Also there are other people, with homes and families to support, who are totally dependent upon the continued prosperity of the group. To suddenly snatch the golden egg away could cause all kinds of financial hardship and heartbreak. Three . . .'

'Oh, lord,' Rhiannon raised her well-shaped eyebrows in despair, 'you'll be bringing on the violins next!'

'This is all fact,' he said doggedly. 'Three,' he held up three stubby fingers, 'Shane is prepared to stay with the group on one condition, and one condition only,' he emphasised, 'that you become his wife. No one else, just you. I suggested Maxine, but he laughed in my face. He's adamant, Rhi, and personally I feel he's making a wise choice. His unease has been building up for months, he needs someone to keep him calm, to put some balance into his life. He had a rotten childhood, and he's very volatile. He needs an anchor.'

'And you expect me to be that anchor,' Rhiannon muttered tetchily.

'Four,' Eddie continued, disregarding her pique, 'if you marry Shane he says he'll stay on for a year, which gives us time to organise auditions, try out several new guys and train up the best of the bunch. Once the new guy's established Shane can leave Submission, you and he divorce, and there's no harm done.'

'It's not unusual to be divorced,' Kim interrupted. 'All my friends are doing it.'

'Except that I, in my innocent way, happen to believe in living happily ever after,' Rhiannon commented drily, as she fidgeted with the collar of her pink angora sweater.

'I'm sure Shane would agree to a year's marriage on a platonic basis,' Eddie continued, blithely ignoring Tony's smothered guffaw from the back seat. 'Suppose I write out a contract this week, and then you can both have a look at it and see what you think? It can be purely a business arrangement. Think how many people's lives you would make secure, and who knows, once you're married you might like it.'

'I'm sure you will,' Kim intruded.

'And Shane might decide to stay with the group after all,' Eddie smiled. 'You really would be doing us all a great favour.'

'It's hardly like sacrificing yourself to the Hunchback of Notre Dame, is it?' giggled Kim.

'More like Bluebeard and Warren Beatty rolled into one,' Rhiannon murmured darkly.

'You'll think it over?' Tony's voice was hopeful.

Her nerves were shattered by the constant pressure of their arguments. 'When we arrive in Glasgow I'll talk to Shane, and we'll try and work something out.'

Eddie exchanged relieved glances with the couple in the back seat.

'Something which does *not* include getting married,' she finished rebelliously.

* * *

The remainder of the journey north was accomplished in peace. They stopped at a motorway service station for a quick lunch, and as they drove on again through the small town of Gretna Green into the border foothills of Scotland, the sun appeared from behind the clouds, and the pale sky deepened into blue. The road wound its way through a valley with forested slopes on one side and fields dotted with newly born spring lambs on the other. The air was fresh and clean, and gradually Rhiannon's headache faded and she began to relax. It was mid-afternoon when they reached Newton Mearns, a smart residential suburb to the south of Glasgow.

'There's the hotel,' Eddie pointed to a solid red sandstone mansion in the midst of manicured parklands. 'We're away from the city centre this time. The pantechnicon should have arrived at the theatre by now, so I'll go up there in an hour or two and check everything out. No work today, folks, I suggest you all take it easy. Don't bother with the mail, Rhi, we'll get stuck into it in the morning when everyone's at rehearsals. We shall be here for three days, two concerts, so the pressure's not too great.'

Rhiannon swung the Granada on to the grey tarmac of the car park, and drew up alongside the Series 7 BMW.

'Shane probably arrived hours ago,' Tony commented as he climbed from the car and stretched his legs. 'He drives like a bat out of hell. I was on an autobahn in Germany with him once, and I thought we were going to break the sound barrier—whew!' He wiped imaginary sweat from his brow.

As they entered the hotel a small group of teenagers came forward, giggling nervously. 'Please could we have your autograph?' asked the ringleader as the girls surrounded Tony. He signed their books goodnaturedly, laughing and joking with them, while Eddie dealt with matters at the reception desk and arranged for the luggage to be taken to their rooms.

'The manager would like a word with you, sir, to

check security arrangements,' the receptionist told him.

'Fine.'

'I'll go up.' Rhiannon collected her key and climbed the stairs. It was a medium sized family hotel, and her room had been decorated with care. It was pretty, with a matching bedspread and curtains in a pink and white floral design, and a thick deep pink carpet. There was an en suite bathroom with pale green and pink accessories, and fluffy towels. The wide windows overlooked a private garden with trimmed hedges, neat lawns and thick, dark fir trees. Square beds, bursting with spring flowers of red and yellow, formed a bright patchwork of colour. A porter delivered her suitcase, and when she had finished unpacking she changed into gold-coloured suede trousers and a cream cashmere sweater. She was washing her face when there was a knock at the door, and the towel was still in her hands as she went to open it. David was stood hesitantly on the threshold.

'Can I discuss something with you?' he asked anxiously. Rhiannon guessed from the look on his face that it would be a favour, and sighed as she hastily finished patting her face dry.

'Not you, too,' she said impatiently. 'I'm fed up with everyone pressurising me, David—give me a break.'

'I don't intend to pressurise you,' he assured her hastily, 'I merely want to make you aware of a few facts.' He pushed his blond hair from his forehead in a nervous gesture. 'We were talking in the car. Shane really means it about leaving the group unless you marry him,' he said slowly, scanning his sister's face for her reaction. 'He made that perfectly plain. He says he can't carry on any longer with the situation as it is.'

Rhiannon sat down at the pine dressing table and drummed her fingers impatiently.

'He's exaggerating.'

David pulled a face. 'Perhaps so, but it really doesn't matter, the point is that he will leave if you don't agree to his wishes.'

'You're all taking this too seriously, making a fuss

about nothing,' she assured him with feigned coolness, her heart beating rapidly inside her as she persuaded herself that Shane surely would relent and release her from this predicament. She took a silver pendant from her jewellery case and fastened the long chain around her neck, then she picked out a pair of silver stud earrings and began to fix them in her ears. David watched apprehensively.

'Please co-operate, Rhi. If he breaks up the group we must say goodbye to being wealthy. The cash will roll over for a while with royalties and such, but we may be forced to pay off the band, and I understand there are tax bills due. If the money stops it also means I must sell Mum and Dad's new house.'

Rhiannon's head jerked up sharply to stare at him in horror.

'I've got a hefty mortgage on it,' he confessed with considerable embarrassment.

'You told me you'd bought it outright!' Rhiannon accused. 'You assured Mum and Dad that everything was taken care of.'

'That was a little white lie. The house was expensive, but I knew how much they'd enjoy living there, and I wanted to make them happy. I never thought there would be any reason why I couldn't keep up the mortgage payments.'

'But Dad's been so much healthier since they moved in—if he realised you were having money troubles he could easily have a relapse. You know his heart isn't strong.'

'Exactly.'

'Oh no!' she wailed, as the implications of the situation hit her. She felt as though she had received a physical blow.

'I suppose they could move into a smaller house,' David suggested tentatively.

'What! After all the pleasure and pride they've taken in you buying the house for them in the first place? It would be a disaster for them to be turned out now.

Can't you economise, David, cut down on your expenses and save the money to pay off the mortgage in a lump sum? I could try and rake up a thousand or so.'

'Thanks, but the odd thousand wouldn't make much difference. I still owe a hell of a sum, and there's something else to consider.'

'What?' Rhiannon was panic-stricken, her world was turning itself rapidly upside down and inside out.

'Cheryl and I want to be married soon and set up home.'

'Surely that could wait? You've only known each other a short while, there's plenty of time. If the group disintegrates you could find another job and get married when you're settled in that.'

'No,' he insisted, 'we want to marry soon.'

'You could wait,' Rhiannon repeated firmly, rankled by his stubbornness.

'I don't want to wait, and besides, Cheryl might be pregnant.'

'Pregnant? Oh, David, you didn't waste much time, did you?'

'Don't say anything to anyone,' he looked apologetic, 'not even to Cheryl, it isn't definite yet, so keep it a secret.'

Rhiannon licked her lips in agitation. Her whole body was trembling.

'This is emotional blackmail,' she muttered unevenly. She looked up at her brother, her brown eyes large and imploring. He leant forward and rumpled her hair.

'Of course, it's entirely up to you. Whatever you decide to do is okay by me.'

She gave a mirthless laugh. 'Oh yes?'

When David departed she slumped down on the bed, her senses reeling from the impact of his words. She shook her head in dismay; there were suddenly so many reasons why it was imperative she should marry Shane. She began to fume inwardly. This dreadful situation was all his fault, how dared he place her in such an unwelcome position? She fingered the pendant around her neck and racked her brains. After half an hour she set her mouth into a determined line. Her plan of action was clear. It was time she and Shane had a showdown. He must be made to realise how unreasonable he was being. His selfish ultimatum was in the process of wrecking her world in less than twenty-four hours. She pulled on beige leather boots and brushed her hair, then made up her face, applying taupe shadow to her eyelids and thickening her long lashes with sooty black mascara. She smeared lip-gloss on her mouth and with a resolute expression strode down the corridor to Shane's room. Briskly she rapped on the door.

'Who is it?'

'Rhiannon.'

Shane raised an amused eyebrow at the tight look on her face as she marched in to sit determinedly in an armchair by the window. He folded his arms and leant casually back against the chest of drawers to study her. He was in a bitter chocolate-coloured crewneck sweater and matching corduroy slacks.

'You obviously mean business.' A grin tugged at the side of his mouth.

'Do you realise what you've done?' she flared, rattled by the innate confidence of his expression. 'Ever since you announced your intention of leaving the group unless we marry I've been under pressure. It's not fair!' Tears sprang unexpectedly into her eyes and her chin quivered. 'You must see you can't go ahead with this ridiculous idea and force me to marry you.'

'I'm not forcing you, there is a choice,' he pointed out calmly.

'Some choice! You're unreasonable.'

He shook his head. 'I'm realistic. I need you in my life, Rhi, if I'm to continue with the group. I can't go it alone much longer or else I really will lose my cool, and that could be disastrous. I don't know why you're making such a fuss—we've known each other a long time, we get on well, and it's patently obvious that the vibrations are there between us.'

'They're not!'

'Oh no?' His mouth twisted into a curl of disbelief. 'However, the bottom line is that I can't continue without some kind of support.'

'So you want me for a crutch!'

He laughed. 'Yes, I do, though it depends what you mean by crutch.'

Rhiannon stood up quickly and looked out of the window with blind eyes. 'Change your mind, Shane,' she pleaded.

'No.' The reply was peremptory.

'You're not playing fair! You told the others you needed me to keep the fans away, but that's not the real reason, is it?'

'Maybe, maybe not, though you must agree they are a nuisance.' He was infuriatingly cool, making her turn her back on him in furious disgust.

'Eddie's told me about Kim's suggestion,' he said. 'I'd be willing to agree to that.'

Rhiannon spun round, wide-eyed in surprise. 'You would?'

'Yes. I agree that the marriage need never be consummated if *you* don't wish it to be, though obviously my feelings differ.' He made a vague gesture. 'But to all outward appearances it must be a loving relationship. Perhaps the fans aren't the paramount reason for my wanting you as my wife, but we must convince them, and the press, that we are happily married.'

Rhiannon chewed her lip, her mind working pellmell as she considered the situation from this new angle.

'Sit down,' Shane said softly. 'Let me try and explain how I feel.'

She sat down again, her large eyes fixed on his face. It seemed as though there was something struggling inside him, unrelenting and restless. He was unhappy and vulnerable, and she felt a rush of sympathy for him which she immediately suppressed.

'It's difficult to know where to start,' he sighed, pushing his hands deep into his pockets. 'I've deliberately never said much about my background because I was afraid some reporter might take up the tale. It would only distress my mother if anything was written about it, and it certainly wasn't her fault I had such an un-settled childhood. I was an only child and a very lonely one, because my parents were continually on the move. My father refused to remain in one place longer than a year or so. We'd move to a new neighbourhood, start to make a few friends and then—wham,' he slapped a fist into the palm of his hand, 'he'd arrive home and an-nounce that we couldn't stay there any longer. Then there'd be tears and angry scenes between him and my mother, and days of general moodiness, but in the end we always had to pack our possessions and set off for the next town, or country. I don't know why he couldn't bear to stay put, perhaps because he was something of a misfit. He was half English, half Filipino, but whatever the reason he was certainly filled with wanderlust. I must have inherited my restless temperament from him! I've moved around so much I really don't know where I belong any more, but I'm going to make an attempt to put down roots. I need to be settled, Rhi,' he said des-perately. 'I'm buying a house in Sussex, and I shall be taking possession soon after the tour ends.'

She looked at him in surprise.

'I know, I've kept quiet about that, too,' he agreed. 'But I've reached the time in life when I want a base. Even if I don't settle in England eventually it's still a good investment. It's a fine house. You'll like it, and we can furnish it together. I've almost finalised the negotia-tions and soon it will be mine—and you'll be mine too.'

He reached down and caught hold of the silver chain around her neck, forcing her to stand close to him. For a still moment he rested his cheek against her forehead, and then his arms encircled her. She pressed both hands against his chest to push him away, but she was trapped. Shane narrowed his blue eyes, and then his mouth was on hers, soft and insistent. Ruthlessly he forced her lips open.

'No, Shane!' she pleaded, fighting against his grasp. His mouth was warm and moist, and inexorably a wave of desire flooded her body and gradually changed her resistance into need. His lips were hot against hers, and the blood pounded at her temples like a jungle rhythm. She thrust her arms around his neck, weaving her fingers among his thick black curls. His hands slid beneath her sweater and up to caress the curves of her full breasts.

'You're beautiful,' he whispered huskily, running his fingertips across her taut nipples and stroking the silken skin. His breath was fiery on her cheek, 'I want you very much. Marry me, my love—it will all work out.'

'No!' Rhiannon stirred impatiently in his arms. Her breasts were so sensitive to his touch, and she was filled with an urgent desire to feel his bare skin against hers.

A sudden loud knocking at the door startled them both, and Rhiannon sprang guiltily away from him, her heart thudding. Shane laughed smugly and reached down to plant a small kiss on the corner of her mouth before he rearranged her sweater and went to open the door.

'Hello, Shane.' Eddie peered in from the corridor. 'Hello, Rhi. Might have guessed you'd be here.' He grinned knowingly, noticing her flushed face and tousled hair. 'How are you two lovebirds, then?'

Rhiannon glared at him, her face stony.

'Oops, sorry, didn't mean to jump the gun!'

As Eddie involved Shane in a busy discussion about a video they were planning, she struggled to calm her trembling body. Throughout the entire conversation she was conscious of Shane glancing at her from time to time in amusement, and she heartily wished she had had the strength to reject his advances. Now his relaxed, confident stance indicated that he took it for granted she would agree to his proposal.

'And another thing,' Eddie finished off, 'there's a group of girls downstairs who've been waiting patiently for over an hour to get your autograph. They refuse to leave until they've seen you.'

Shane uttered an oath.

'It's good public relations,' Eddie wheedled.

Shane's face darkened. 'Girls—always bloody girls! You know as well as I do that if I sign for this crowd there'll be another gaggle waiting five minutes later,' he clenched and unclenched his fists as he swung between co-operation and his own need for privacy.

'Why don't you go down and sign?' Rhiannon suggested. 'It'll only take a few minutes—it's not much to ask.'

Shane looked at her thoughtfully and pursed his lips. 'Tell you what, how about you and me motoring to Largs? It's on the coast, not too far from here. We can have dinner there, and I'll see the girls on our way out.'

She sighed. Nothing was straightforward with Shane, he insisted on trading with her emotions and bartering his way along. 'Very well,' her voice was resigned.

'Great!' he smiled triumphantly. 'Go and put on something warm, it'll be cold by the sea.' He took a tan leather jacket from the wardrobe and slung it casually across his shoulders. His surliness had disappeared completely. 'Give Rhi a minute and we'll be down,' he assured Eddie.

As she collected a red fox fur jacket from her room Rhiannon looked at herself in the mirror. Her face appeared remarkably composed, considering her mind and body were in a state of utter confusion. Shane had, once again, reduced her to a willing accomplice, within seconds, and she was disgusted with herself. It was difficult to believe that her body said 'yes' so directly to his touch, when her mind was protesting 'no' with equal firmness. If she was going to come to an arrangement with him it was imperative she did so under her own terms. There was no way she was prepared to surrender completely to his selfish demands.

Shane signed the autograph books pleasantly enough, though the determined set of his jaw indicated that he was not prepared to be too amenable. He was not the kind of man who enjoyed casual gossip with strangers, albeit adoring ones. He made a point of keeping Rhiannon close and slipped an arm around her shoulders as, the signing completed, they walked to the car. The group of girls stood and watched them, and waved delightedly in response to Shane's hesitant salute of farewell as he thrust the car out on to the road. Rhiannon snapped on her seat-belt.

'Don't you trust me?' he queried with a grin, his hands firm and competent on the wheel.

'Never. You've placed me in an impossible position. There must be some other way out—getting married is too drastic. Wouldn't you consider staying on for a year with Submission until they find a replacement?' Her voice softened. 'Surely you could survive for a year? Please, Shane!'

He glanced at her, merriment flecking his gaze. 'And what would you offer by way of an inducement?' His voice was low and suggestive, and Rhiannon flushed. His tone made it perfectly clear what he meant.

'I'll be your girl-friend and loving towards you in public,' she offered wildly.

Shane put his hand on her thigh. 'It's what happens in private that concerns me,' he said quietly.

She removed his hand, and he returned it to the wheel without comment.

'Surely you could manage for another year?' She was fully aware she was grasping at straws.

Shane's face hardened into a bleak, altogether alien appearance, 'Let's stop playing games,' he snapped. 'It's as simple as this—unless you agree to marry me I shall leave Submission immediately. It's your decision.'

'That's what David said,' she wailed, 'but it's not. It's your damned decision and you know it! You've backed me into a corner and there's no way out.'

'But you'll like being in a corner with me, I promise you,' he cast a shrewd glance at her distressed profile. 'Have you ever been to the west coast of Scotland before?' He deftly changed the topic of conversation, making Rhiannon grit her teeth in annoyance, maddened by his evasive tactics.

'No, have you?'

'Often. I lived near Glasgow for a while when I was a kid. We used to spend Sundays in Largs, walking along the shore and eating fabulous ice cream sundaes.'

'How many different places have you lived in?' she asked in a voice which was carefully formal, as she smouldered over his refusal to continue the discussion about her future and that of Submission. He seemed to think it was a straightforward matter, but it wasn't, and he was too manipulative by half.

'I was born in England, but shortly afterwards we moved to the States, then up to Canada, and back to California. When I was five we emigrated to Australia and lived in Sydney. Later Dad shipped us across to New Zealand, and later back to Scotland, England and so on,' he waved a hand dismissively. 'It was only when my father died that we returned to England for good. I was sixteen at the time. My mother is English to the backbone, and she couldn't wait to return. Fortunately she had some private money of her own and was able to buy a house. I don't know how she coped with those years of compulsive travelling. All her married life she never stayed anywhere long enough to make a place for herself in a community, or develop any close friendships. It really soured their marriage. She and Dad used to fight like mad, but she always stuck by him in the end— I suppose deep down she loved him. She used to plead with him to stop running so that we could have a settled existence, and so that my education wouldn't suffer. Oddly enough I still managed to achieve decent exam results despite all the different schools.'

'And you never discovered why your father had always to be on the move?' Rhiannon's temper had subsided as she listened with interest to Shane's description of his childhood.

'No, he was a very secretive man. I'm sure there was a mystery at the back of it all, but after he died my mother clammed up and refused to talk about him, so

I've never discovered the truth. I imagine he'd worn her out during the years of travelling and she needed to obliterate the unhappy memories. She's delighted to be settled back in England. She married again, a couple of years ago, and she made damned sure her new husband wasn't a wanderer. All she wants now is to stay in the same place for the rest of her life.'

'But what about you? What do you want to do?'

'I don't know,' he rubbed at his brow. 'There are several loose ends which I need to tie up before I can finally put down roots. I spent the first sixteen years of my life on the move, and it's a difficult habit to break. I still have a touch of wanderlust, but perhaps it will fade. I'd love to know more about my father and what moti-vated him.'

'Why don't you go to the Philippines and visit his family?' Rhiannon suggested.

He shrugged. 'Perhaps I will some day. I might dis-cover I belong there, it could be like going back home, who knows? However, for the time being I shall concen-trate on the house in Sussex, it's the first property I've ever owned.'

The afternoon was fading as they drove down the long hill into Largs, and the glow of the setting sun touched the trees and hedgerows with gold, giving them a magical mellowness. The sky was a clear, crystalline blue. Shane halted the car at the far end of the long promenade and turned to look at her.

'Shall we have a walk along the shore? Largs is a town people retire to, it's full of old age pensioners, so with any luck we should escape attention.'

Rhiannon nodded and climbed from the car, grate-fully pulling her fur jacket around her, for the late afternoon air was as cold as ice cream against her face. Silently Shane interlaced his fingers with hers. 'That's the Isle of Arran,' he pointed to hazy violet mountains across the water. 'Are you warm enough?'

'I'm fine. Tell me more about your father—what kind of work did he do?' They started to walk.

'Anything that came along, I guess. Obviously a structured career was out of the question. Sometimes he had a job as a salesman, sometimes he did clerical work, or laboured on building sites. He tried to avoid that, though, he didn't like rough work because it messed up his hands. He was a concert pianist by profession, and a damn good one too. He could have found work with any top class orchestra if he'd tried, he had classical training as a boy, but he absolutely refused to perform in public. He had an obsession about never drawing attention to himself—obviously something of that has rubbed off on me,' he added with an ironic lift of his brow.

'Did he teach you to play the piano?'

He nodded. 'Music was the one constant feature of my childhood. My father started teaching me when I was very young. Wherever we were we always had a piano around, it was the only thing that kept Dad sane. He would play for hours, concerto after concerto—it was a release for him, but it used to drive my mother wild!' He squeezed her fingers. 'I'm arranging for the music room to be soundproofed at the house in Sussex. You'll not be driven to distraction when . . .' he paused significantly, '*if* you live there.'

Rhiannon grew tense as she remembered his scheming, and he chuckled at the annoyance flickering across her brow. 'Cheer up, we're having a great time, so don't start looking stormy again.' She held the collar of the fur jacket around her head to keep away the cold wind. Her lips were soft and full, and her face troubled. Shane looked down at her steadily. 'You're lovely.' His voice was low. He kissed the tip of her nose. 'Don't worry. We can make each other very happy. If anyone can persuade me to settle down, it's you.'

She turned from him and continued walking along the stony shore, deep in thought. The wind was whipping up choppy waves on the sea and in the distance dark grey clouds were beginning to gather. Shane strode along beside her, kicking the occasional pebble haphazardly into the sea. Rhiannon kept her eyes on the shore, her long hair blowing about her like a shiny brown banner. The beach and promenade were deserted, the chill wind had driven everyone indoors.

She bit her lip, trying to stifle the darts of alarm that pricked unceasingly as she considered his proposition. It was vital she consider everything coolly and logically, though she was tempted to turn her back and walk away—and say to hell with Shane, and everyone else. Why shouldn't she put herself first? She was a skilled secretary. She could easily find another job—one in a less demanding profession, engineering perhaps. That surely would not be so high-powered, so emotionally charged as the entertainment world. After all, she had stumbled into show business purely by chance, she could easily retreat and go back to normality, away from the fans and reporters—and Shane.

But that would be selfish. She was needed. Eddie needed her if he was to achieve his life's ambitions. David needed her to help repay their parents for their undemanding sacrifices. Her father, particularly, needed her if he was to enjoy a secure and peaceful retirement in good health. And finally, though she wasn't quite sure why, *Shane* needed her. For a long time they walked together in silence, then she stopped abruptly.

'I'll marry you, but never forget that you've forced me to submit.'

Shane watched her warily, the determined look on her face warning him to tread carefully. He waited.

'It must be on my terms,' she continued, swallowing hard. 'It must be a business arrangement. Eddie can write out a contract. The marriage will last for one year, and then we divorce. I'm prepared to be your wife in public and be devoted enough to fool everyone, but it's purely a façade. A year should give Eddie sufficient time to find a replacement. It's a business arrangement, Shane,' she stressed. 'You understand?'

He nodded his dark head.

'Take it or leave it,' Rhiannon said.

'You mean take *you* or leave *you*.' There was an ironical twist to his mouth. Rhiannon bent down to pick a flat grey stone from the shore. She sent it skimming away across the water.

'Yes, I suppose so,' she agreed in a small voice.

'Then I'll take you,' he replied firmly. 'Let's go and find somewhere to eat.'

Everyone who knew about the arrangement was delighted with her acquiescence. It was as though Rhiannon had provided the winning ticket for a million-dollar lottery, but the lavish gratitude which was showered upon her grated. In the midst of all the celebrating the fact that she had been forced to sacrifice a year of her life was forgotten. David's pleasure was particularly enthusiastic.

'That's great news,' he grinned. 'Now that everything is back to normal I can pay off the mortgage gradually and save towards Cheryl and me getting hitched. I promise I'll try to economise and not be so rash in future. Eddie will start auditioning for a new guy as soon as we return to London.'

'But what about me?' yelped Rhiannon. 'My life's not back to normal. It's going to be decidedly *ab*normal from now on!'

'What are you complaining about? Most girls would give their right arm to marry Shane,' David said pointedly.

'It's a business arrangement, nothing else,' she muttered grimly through her teeth.

'Don't go spreading that around. It must appear as though you really love each other, any suspicion of it not being a real marriage and the press will be on to you. Those reporters are like a flock of vultures, longing for a juicy scandal. If it was discovered you and Shane were only pretending, that would really turn on the heat!'

The Glasgow concerts were a crowning finale for the tour. The audiences cheered loud and long, and despite flanks of navy-coated policemen clearing a path, the car carrying the group from the theatre after the show could only inch its way through the press of fans. They flattened themselves against the car windows, giggling and knocking on the glass.

'Thank goodness that's over,' breathed Shane as eventually the car gathered speed. 'One day some teenager will get run over, or be trampled on, or perhaps they'll all run amok and it'll end up in mass rape.'

'You should be so lucky!' laughed David. 'It's a frightening thought, though. Fans are fine in small groups, but en masse they can be terrifying.'

'I don't need fans, period,' Shane snapped.

The wedding was arranged for three weeks later at an unobtrusive register office on the outskirts of London. Eddie had drawn up a contract which they both found acceptable, and they had signed their agreement. Rhiannon was relieved to possess a written document, it placed everything strictly on a business footing. She agreed to live in Shane's house and act as his loving bride in public. He had tried to include some kind of financial security for her at the end of the twelve months, but she had strongly objected.

'You're not buying me, Shane, I'm not a whore!'

He had rounded on her with an icy ferocity that made her recoil. 'Don't say that! I just don't want you to suffer in any way.'

'Don't you?' she asked bitterly, and he had turned on his heel and walked from the room, his face dark and troubled.

Rhiannon's parents, like everyone else, were thrilled to hear news of the impending wedding. She felt distinctly uncomfortable at deceiving them about the true circumstances, but it was vital that as few people as possible were aware of the arrangement.

She and Shane had met her parents at the station and driven them to her flat, where they would stay until after the wedding.

'What a good-looking young man,' her mother had said delightedly when Shane had left. 'You're a lucky girl. He thinks the world of you—he's so attentive. He's just as charming as Brad was. Isn't it appropriate, him taking over Brad's position in the group, and now the two of you falling in love. It's like history repeating itself.'

Rhiannon bit back a tart reply, and bent her head, seemingly engrossed in pressing the cream linen suit which she would wear for the ceremony. She looked down at the naked third finger of her left hand and rubbed it thoughtfully. Soon she would be wearing a wide golden wedding band. She had refused to accept an engagement ring from Shane. She didn't want a second one, she had decided with unshakeable perversity. She still had Brad's ring, tucked away in a scarlet brocade sachet in her jewellery case. It was only an insignificant diamond cluster, bought in the days before Submission had hit the big time, but she didn't want anything bigger and better that Shane would be sure to buy. She was trying hard to cling on to her loyalty to Brad, but it was becoming increasingly difficult. Shane was *here* and *now*. He was definitely not a man to entertain a rival, especially a mere memory. His anger at her refusal of a ring had made her wonder if he had guessed at her obscure reasoning, and his despairing look of resignation had made her feel guilty, but she had not relented.

The previous evening, however, he had unexpectedly appeared at the flat, and after chatting with her parents and Anne, her flatmate, he had followed Rhiannon out into the kitchen when she went to make coffee.

'For you.' He handed her a small crimson velvet box. When she opened it she saw a brilliant solitaire diamond on a slender gold chain.

'It's beautiful!' she gasped, lifting it out. 'But I can't accept it.'

'Yes, you can,' he told her firmly. 'Turn round and let me fasten it for you.' Rhiannon lifted the thick fall of hair at the back of her neck, while Shane fixed the catch.

'You're going to be my wife, remember?' he insisted softly into her ear. When the chain was secure he placed his hands firmly on her shoulders and rubbed his clean-shaven cheek slowly against hers. The scent of his after-shave filled her nostrils, and Rhiannon stiffened, for already his touch was beginning to upset her equilibrium.

'I want to buy gifts for you, people will consider it odd if I don't.' He swung her round to face him. 'And now you must kiss me to say thank you, *as though you mean it*.' He took hold of her face in both hands and kissed her deeply. As his breathing quickened his mouth became desperate and searching, as though he needed to absorb all of her. Rhiannon's nerve ends pulsated, and all common sense disappeared. Her carefully constructed good intentions of remaining cool and calm, and emotionally aloof, vanished and instinctively she thrust herself against him, returning the heat of his kiss. His hands began to slide down her body.

'We're not in public now,' she said unevenly, trying to break away, but he refused to let her go.

'We have to put on a show for your parents—you must see that,' he muttered hoarsely. 'What better way to convince them we're genuinely in love than to have you returning to the living room all pink and tumbled, with a satisfied smile on your face?' His grin brimmed with masculine superiority. Slowly, sensuously, he brushed his lips backwards and forwards across her brow. 'Relax, my love,' he crooned. 'You know you want me as much as I want you.'

'I don't,' Rhiannon denied uncertainly.

Shane pulled down the corners of his mouth in dis-belief. She turned her head, but he caught hold of her jaw in his fingers and held her firm. Gently he kissed her nose, her eyelids and again her lips. He was an ex-perienced lover, and although she knew his expertise had been gained through his contact with many women her skin began to throb with the unceasing pressure of his lips and the touch of his fingertips. He traced a slow, erotic path down her throat to the vee of her tartan shirt.

'No, Shane,' she moaned softly, as his hands slid beneath the soft cotton, but his strong fingers never faltered in their determined path to her breasts.

'Is that coffee ready yet?' her father called from the living room, and for a moment Shane hesitated in his onslaught. Rhiannon seized her chance, and tore herself from his grasp, fastening her shirt with shaking fingers.

His low laugh was supremely confident. 'That's better, you look delightfully pink and tumbled now.'

'And satisfied?' she asked, rapidly taking the cups and saucers from the shelves.

'I doubt it,' he said, leaning back, his hands clasped behind his neck. 'I'm certainly not. Thank God, it won't be long before we shall be alone together in Sussex.'

'It's a business arrangement!' she shrieked. 'You agreed!'

Shane put a finger to his lips. 'Not so loud, everyone'll hear.'

'We only have to pretend we care for each other *in public*,' she hissed frantically.

'So I'm allowed to make love to you in the middle of Trafalgar Square, but not alone in bed, is that it?' The smirk on his handsome face indicated his amusement.

'You're impossible!' Rhiannon snapped, as she put the milk jug and sugar bowl on to a tray.

'No, I'm not. I won't make you do anything you don't want to do. I admit I shall certainly try and persuade you to see things my way, but I'd never force you, that's not my scene at all. However, the prospect of two hot-blooded people like you and me living together under the same roof on a platonic basis is most unlikely.'

'No, it's not,' retorted Rhiannon, blushing furiously. 'And I'm not hot-blooded!'

'Aren't you?' Shane asked archly.

CHAPTER FOUR

DURING the three weeks before the wedding they had met only briefly and always in the company of others. Rhiannon had spent long hours at the office in an attempt to clear a backlog of work and to train one of the secretaries who would take over her duties. It had been agreed that after her marriage she would only go into the office on a casual basis, whenever Shane was working in London, as it was too far to commute daily. The weekends she had spent busily shopping for her trousseau, and packing her belongings for them to be transported down to Sussex. Already wedding presents from friends and fans were pouring in, and she had tried hard to keep up to date with the long list of 'thank you' letters which had to be written. By night-time she was exhausted, and had dropped into bed and fallen asleep immediately.

She was grateful for the rush and bustle, for she didn't want time to think, and she didn't want to be alone with Shane. His presence only made her dwell on the falseness of her marriage, but fortunately he, too, was occupied, moving from his London apartment to the house. On the odd occasions when they had been together he had treated her with a fond sensuality which had left her senses reeling. He appeared to feel no qualms of conscience over the ruthless way he had engineered their relationship—indeed, on the contrary, he was in the very best of moods. It was only when he was asked to discuss publicity for the major London concert that his affability wavered, to be replaced by brittle resignation.

They had chosen the small register office in an attempt to avoid flocks of fans. Shane clung stubbornly to the hope that they would be married quietly, but Rhiannon doubted it. There was rarely a celebrity wedding which went unnoticed, and she accepted the likelihood that crowds would gather. It was a happy surprise, therefore, to discover only a handful of spectators when the limousine, carrying herself and her father, drew up outside the steps to the register office.

Her stomach twisted into a tight knot as she climbed out, and her face was noticeably pale. She looked elegant and remote in her tailored linen suit, but inside she was a mass of nerves and contradictions. The spray of white freesia pinned to her lapel was echoed by a cluster on the white grosgrain ribbon around her fine straw hat. Her thick chestnut hair had been swept back into a sophisticated chignon, and the solitaire diamond sparkled at her throat. Shane came down the steps to meet her, and Rhiannon's heart lurched. He looked incredibly mature and sombre, his dark grey suit and dazzling white shirt making him look far more like a business executive than a pop star. His long black hair had been cut to barely brush the collar of his jacket, and the romantic musketeer had disappeared, to be replaced by a svelte man of the world. His blue eyes burned in the taut planes of his face, and Rhiannon was surprised to feel his hand tremble as he closed it about hers.

'Thank God you've come!' he breathed as they entered the building. 'I was terrified in case you had second thoughts.'

Rhiannon smiled uncertainly. She went through the entire ceremony in a dream. Everything seemed unreal, as though it was happening to someone else, though she was aware of answering the questions automatically. Before she knew it, she and Shane were man and wife, being ushered out into the sunshine for photographs. She raised her hand to shield her eyes from the brightness. The ranks of spectators had swelled and there was a loud cheer as they emerged.

Shane swore under his breath when he noticed the phalanx of cameras clicking away.

'Give her a kiss!' shouted a photographer. For an instant Rhiannon thought he was going to refuse, but he turned and kissed her briefly on the cheek.

'We're not performing dogs,' he growled. 'Let's go.' The crowds spread between them and the waiting car at the bottom of the steps. Shane strode forward, holding Rhiannon's hand tightly.

'Wait a minute, boyo!' yelled a second cameraman. 'We've a job to do. What about giving your new wife a real sexy kiss, to please the young ladies?' A cheer from the crowd reinforced his request. Shane shifted his broad shoulders uneasily beneath his dark suit, and his muscles tightened, like a wild animal ready to spring. He glared at the row of photographers. Tentatively Rhiannon reached out her hand and touched his cheek. Startled, he looked at her, reading the intention in her eyes, and she raised her head and kissed him. He remained still and rigid, but then the touch of her lips made him forget the spectators and his arms closed around her. His mouth became urgent and Rhiannon could feel the excitement begin to grow within him. It was only when the crowds began to applaud that he pulled away and grinned sheepishly. She couldn't help laughing at his unusual lack of composure, it was not like Shane to be bemused. Suddenly he gave a chuckle, lifted her off her feet and swung her round in a spontaneous joyous whirl. The crowds laughed and the cameras clicked. He set her down again, gave her a resounding kiss, and then together they ran happily down the steps, through the crowds and into the waiting car. As the fans clustered round a girl pushed her head through the open window and thrust a silver cardboard horseshoe at them. As Shane accepted it Rhiannon realised the girl was Betsy. Shane reached out and squeezed her hand, making her blush with pleasure. 'I wish you both the best of luck,' she beamed. It was only when they were driving away to the reception that Rhiannon remembered there had been no further communications from Shane's number one fan since the confrontation in Manchester.

'In another couple of miles you'll be at your new home, Rhiannon Santiago.' Shane glanced obliquely across at her profile, but it was too dark to gauge any reaction as she sat silently beside him in the speeding car. It had been mid-evening when, amidst much jocularity, they had finally detached themselves from the reception at the five-star hotel. A quick stop in the back streets had given them the opportunity to remove bawdy stickers and confetti from the car, much to the amusement of passersby, and now it was late. They were deep in the countryside, and for the past half hour had been driving along narrow, twisty lanes. The moon had long disappeared behind clouds, and the night was black, only the pale yellow beams of the powerful headlights indicated their way. On either side of the road hedgerows grew thick and tall, fragrant with blossoms. Shane drove quickly and expertly, his concentration leaving little time for conversation.

Rhiannon was grateful for time to sit and think. She had been surprised to find herself wholeheartedly enjoying the reception. Everyone was happy about their marriage, and naturally expected her to be so too. Shane's good humour had been infectious, and she had thrust aside her doubts to respond easily to his affection. She had to admit it hadn't been difficult. He seemed genuinely delighted to have her as his wife, and she knew everyone had been deceived into believing they were very much in love. But now the exhilaration was slipping away, leaving her ill at ease. She had kept her part of the agreement in public, it remained to be seen whether he would keep his in private. Involuntarily she shivered with apprehension, and Shane noticed a sudden upward tilt of her chin. He thrust his foot on the brake pedal to slide the big car smoothly between two grey stone gateposts and along a short gravel drive, before pulling to a stop.

'I hope you approve.' There was a flicker of anxiety in his deep voice. Rhiannon climbed from the car and looked up at the black and white timbered house—her new home. At that moment the moon appeared from behind fast-moving clouds and a silvery light illuminated the building. In the muted gleam she was able to decipher attractive leaded light windows, a leafy creeper twisting its way to the second storey, and a heavy oak door.

'It's charming,' she said. 'I'm longing to have a proper look around in the morning.'

Shane unlocked the front door, and putting one arm around her shoulders and another behind her knees, picked her up easily. 'I must carry you over the threshold, it's traditional,' he grinned, striding with her into the hall, every inch the loving bridegroom. Still holding her, he awkwardly stretched out a hand and switched on the light. Rhiannon blinked in the sudden brightness. Her arms were around his neck, her face only inches from his. Tendrils of her hair, loosened from the chignon, brushed against his cheek, and he could smell the musky fragrance of her perfume. He smiled, almost shyly, and spontaneously she kissed him.

'Two unsolicited kisses in one day,' he murmured drily. 'I'm doing well!' He gazed at her, a soft look in his blue eyes which made her heart keel over, and then abruptly he set her down. 'I'll bring the cases from the car.'

While Shane was occupied Rhiannon explored the ground floor. It was her first visit to the house, and she recalled how he had explained that originally it had been a seventeenth-century tithe barn, but had been lavishly modernised, retaining its old-world charm, but adding sophistications from the twentieth century. There was a spacious lounge with oak beams in the ceiling, a brick feature wall with inglenook and log fire, and wide French windows which opened out on to a stone-flagged patio. On the far side of the hall was a room which Shane had obviously chosen to be his music room, for its only contents were a piano, piled high with music scores, and a stool. Through an archway towards the rear of the house was a formal dining room, and a kitchen with dining alcove. The entire ground floor and stairs were covered with a rich, creamy-coloured carpet, but the rooms were sparsely furnished, and looked bare with uncurtained windows and naked walls.

'I've put the suitcases in the bedrooms,' he said, coming downstairs to join her. 'Have you had a look around? What do you think?'

'It's lovely,' she assured him again with a smile. 'It has tremendous potential. When it's properly furnished and decorated it will be beautiful.'

'That's what I thought. If I have a comfortable home perhaps it will make me put down roots.'

'But then again, the house might only be a temporary possession, like me,' she pointed out lightly, playing some kind of unfair game which only served to make her feel dissatisfied with herself.

Shane ignored her. 'I haven't much furniture of my own. The apartment I rented in London came fully equipped, so we'll virtually be starting from scratch. There are curtains in the bedrooms, however, for the sake of modesty. I've put the boxes you sent over up in the spare bedroom. There's a pile of wedding presents too, we can unpack them tomorrow.'

'The carpets are well cared for—I didn't know you were a virtuoso with a vacuum cleaner,' she teased, looking around.

'I'm not. I've arranged for a woman from the village to come in for a few hours each day, a Mrs Jackson. She's a hard worker and very pleasant. She's been cleaning the windows and generally keeping things shipshape. She has a teenage son, Alan, and he's been helping out in the garden, mowing the lawns and doing some weeding.' He gave her a long look. 'Can I get you a drink? There's coffee, tea and some brandy.'

'No, thanks,' she yawned. 'It's late and I'm tired. Please will you show me where my bedroom is?'

Shane bolted the front door and together they mounted the stairs. Rhiannon was acutely aware of him walking behind her. It felt as though the two of them were alone in the whole world, and her skin prickled in agitation.

'That's the main bedroom, it has an adjoining bathroom,' Shane explained. 'You'll find your suitcase in there.'

'Goodnight,' she said, a little more abruptly than she meant to, and went smartly into the bedroom before he could attempt to kiss her goodnight. Her nerves were taut. The reality of being alone in the house with him was overwhelming. She closed the bedroom door and leant against it, her pulses racing. There was no bolt, but then she wondered whether, if there had been, she would have used it. It was churlish to be so much on her guard. She was suddenly annoyed with her own unfairness—after all, Shane had assured her he would not force his attentions on her, and she had no reason to disbelieve him. Probably by now he was settling down to sleep in his own room. Rhiannon was surprised to feel a stab of chagrin at the thought.

She closed the heavy brocade curtains and undressed quickly, slipping into the silk nightgown which Anne, her flatmate, had insisted she bought for her trousseau. She felt a trifle foolish, alone in the bedroom, wearing the outrageously sexy nightgown, and remembered the day when she and Anne had gone on a shopping spree.

'It's so seductive,' Anne had drooled, fingering the fine coffee coloured lace, 'Shane won't be able to resist you in it. Look at those delicate shoestring straps and the deep bodice—it's beautiful! Mind you, if he's as lusty as he appears to be, I reckon he'll have it off you in five minutes flat!' Anne had winked.

Rhiannon washed her face, cleaned her teeth, and walked back into the bedroom to find her hairbrush. As she was bending over the suitcase the door opened and Shane walked in, fully dressed. She straightened up in surprise.

'Don't you think you should knock?' she asked acidly.

'Why should I?' he drawled. 'It's my house and you *are* my wife.'

'In public!'

'Legally!'

There was no disputing that. She turned to him warily, instantly on the defensive. Already he appeared to be altering the arrangement. She started to speak, but the look in his eyes when he saw her in the lace nightgown silenced her.

'You're beautiful,' he breathed, his eyes ravishing her body. He viewed her with obvious pleasure, the boldness of his gaze making Rhiannon want to cover herself with her hands. She began to grow pink beneath his eyes.

'What do you want, Shane?' Her voice was tart. He looked at her stupidly, then shook his head as though bringing himself to his senses. He cleared his throat before speaking.

'Can you unfasten this cufflink?' He thrust out his arm and she tugged at the heavy silver cufflink with nervous fingers. His masculine closeness threatened her, but she knew, in that moment, that she was in more danger from the desires of her own body than from Shane. With a beating heart and a deliberately casual gesture she dropped the offending cufflink into his palm.

'And this one,' he gestured unseeingly towards his other wrist. She noticed the thick, dark, glinting hairs on the back of his hands. His piercing blue eyes, with their fringe of black lashes, never left her. She felt as though they were suspended in time, and the outside world ceased to exist. She was growing weak from his proximity, her whole being acutely sensitive to his masculinity. He took the second cufflink from her and dropped it, and its partner, uncaringly on to the bedroom carpet.

'Undo your hair,' he commanded. Wordlessly Rhiannon released the elegant chignon and the heavy chestnut hair fell in loose, swirling waves around her shoulders. Shane reached out and pulled her possessively towards him. He kissed her lingeringly. Rhiannon knew she was acting foolishly, but she could no longer control the needs of her body as hot sheets of passion swept over her like flames. She gave her mouth to his demands. Then his fingers pulled at the delicate straps of her nightgown. 'Take it off,' he muttered thickly into her hair, 'I want to look at you.'

Rhiannon sighed, submitting willingly. The nightgown slipped to the floor, brushing softly against her hip and thigh. A dim voice at the back of her mind reminded her that Anne had been wrong—Shane had removed the nightgown in less than five minutes. He looked down at her, his eyes heavy-lidded with desire, and led her to the bed. He lay down beside her, watching as the dark nipples began to harden, then he cupped her breasts in his hands, teasing the taut pinnacles until Rhiannon moaned softly. He kissed her hair, her ears, her mouth, and then, so slowly, as though savouring the delight, he traced the curve of her jaw and throat with his lips until eventually his mouth closed over her breast. She trembled, her body pulsating with desire, and pulled urgently at the buttons of his shirt. Shane paused momentarily to thrust it from him before his mouth returned to her body. His skin was fiery against hers, and his breathing deep and uneven. Slowly, sensuously, he stroked her breasts, then his hand moved down to the tangled mat of dark curls between her thighs. Rhiannon arched her back and shuddered, her body drenched with a desperate sweetness. She tugged at Shane's belt until his hands joined hers, then he was free of his clothes. She rubbed her fingers amongst the thick, dark hair on his chest, moaning at the thrill of his lips, his tongue, his fingers.

'This will be the best lovemaking you've ever had,' he groaned, as her hands slid down his body, caressing the golden skin and the hard muscles which quivered at her touch.

'I'm a virgin,' Rhiannon whispered into his neck.

'What?'

'A virgin.'

'Oh, my God, no!' There was a long, fraught silence.
'A virgin bride—that's the last thing I expected,' he
muttered, and his fingers abruptly deserted her feverish
body. He rolled away from her and lay on his stomach,
his head in his hands. His muscular body trembled with
frustration. Rhiannon had been abandoned. She lay
beside him, her mind whirling, her body throbbing relentlessly with the need of fulfilment. Then she stretched
out a hand and tentatively touched the thick curls at the
nape of his neck.

'Don't!' he barked, and she drew back in fright. His
mood had changed completely. He was no longer a
lover, instead a hostile stranger lay beside her.

'Why didn't you tell me?' he accused, his face bleak
as he turned to glare at her. 'I had no idea. I presumed
you and Brad had made love.'

'What difference does it make?' Rhiannon asked, her
heart fluttering. 'I don't understand.'

'It makes all the difference,' he snapped. 'I'm not
making love to you if you're a virgin. I'm fully aware
that I steam-rollered you into marrying me, but I
honestly had no idea you were . . .' he paused, 'untouched. You're so passionate—God, when we touch
sparks fly! You must be the only twenty-five-year-old
virgin in the whole of the United Kingdom—quite a
rarity!'

'So what!' Rhiannon shot back, stung by his tone.
His rejection of her was humiliating, and she watched in
despairing silence as he swung his long legs over the
side of the bed and pulled on his clothes. It was obvious
he had no intention of continuing their lovemaking, and
she marvelled at his control. She slipped between the
sheets and pulled them up to her neck, covering her
naked body.

'Apparently all the goodtime girls you've had affairs
with have been the kind who jump into bed with anyone,
but I'm not like that. I have principles,' she protested.

'Perhaps I'm old-fashioned, but I don't see the joy in sleeping around—making love should be accompanied by the emotion of love.'

Shane raised two thick eyebrows and grunted. 'You can't tell me Brad didn't have a damn good try to get you into bed,' he said nastily, his eyes glittering like smashed ice.

'Of course he did!' Rhiannon threw the answer back at him. 'We both wanted to make love and were often close to it—after all, we were both very much *in* love. It was a difficult decision, but we happened to believe in the sanctity of marriage and we decided to wait.'

'You make me feel a real bastard,' Shane muttered, moving towards the door.

'*You are!*' She thrust herself roughly down deeper in the bed. 'You forced me into this marriage because of your selfishness, and now you don't know what you want.'

He stopped and twisted towards her, his face hard and angry. 'I know damn well what I want—*you!*' he snarled. 'But the whole situation has changed. Okay, so I was ruthless enough to manoeuvre you into signing the agreement, but I do have some standards. I'm not completely amoral, and I'm certainly not going to force you to give yourself to me on a temporary basis. I'll have to think this out and decide what to do. Goodnight.'

As he closed the door behind him tears of frustration trickled down Rhiannon's cheeks on to the pillow, and she thrust her fist against her mouth to keep from sobbing out loud in rage and misery. She didn't know why she should be so distraught—surely she should have been grateful to escape Shane's lovemaking, which he had so obviously planned? But nothing made sense any more. She resented the brutal way Shane had forced her to marry him, and common sense told her it was wise for their relationship to remain on a platonic level, and yet, and yet ... His lovemaking had awakened a desperate need, and her emotions were clouding the issue as, if she was honest, they had done from the very beginning. She knew, deep down, that there was no way she would have married him if she hadn't been strongly attracted to him. Perhaps, she thought ruefully, she had wanted him to possess her all along and had used the agreement as a convenient smokescreen. She wriggled uncomfortably, her thoughts in confusion. Shane, at least, had made it clear from the start what he expected—but now he had changed his mind. She turned over fretfully and caught sight of the coffee-coloured folds of the silk nightgown discarded on the floor. How ironical it was that she had pretended to herself that Shane would never see her in it. Now he had, but he probably never would again.

She was awakened by his brisk knock on the bedroom door the following morning.

'It's after nine, Rhi,' Shane shouted cheerfully. 'Come and have breakfast.' His voice was annoyingly normal and friendly. Rhiannon washed and pulled on white denim stretch jeans and a soft lilac-coloured sweat-shirt. She twisted her hair up on to the top of her head into a heavy bun and tied it with a lavender ribbon. Her heart thudded painfully in her breast as she went into the kitchen.

'Not much choice, I'm afraid,' Shane smiled. 'Fruit, toast and coffee. We must go shopping today and stock up the larder. Perhaps you could have a look around after breakfast and make a list of the things we need— I've not a clue about housekeeping.' He was buoyantly cheerful, and she found it difficult to believe he was the same man who had rejected her so angrily the previous night.

'I'll do that,' she assured him, matching her mood to his. If this was the way he wanted to play it, that was fine by her. The next move was up to him. She sat down at the table in the dining area, where breakfast was already prepared.

'You must have been up early,' she commented.

'I couldn't sleep,' he said briefly, his eyes avoiding

hers as he reached for the milk jug. 'Mrs Jackson will be here soon, she comes at ten.'

They sat in silence as they ate, the atmosphere strained.

'I've been thinking,' Shane took a gulp of hot coffee, 'you were right all along, it's far better to keep our relationship platonic as it's a temporary thing. It was selfish of me to expect anything else, and I'm sorry. I was so determined to have my own way that I never considered the implications. I admire you for having scruples. You're right, sleeping around does make you despise yourself in the long run—I should know.' He raised a derisive brow. 'If you want our marriage to end here and now I shall understand.'

Rhiannon looked down into her coffee cup. She was aware it had taken an immense effort for him to admit his mistakes. He was a proud man, and seldom apologised for anything. She also knew she wanted him, whatever the rights and wrongs of the marriage, whatever the terms he stipulated. Slowly she raised her eyes to his.

'Don't look at me like that,' he muttered, shaking his head. 'You're so bloody beautiful, how am I to resist you?'

The knowledge that he, too, was finding the situation fraught made her suddenly lighthearted.

'With difficulty?' she enquired, a smile playing on her lips.

'With much difficulty.'

'I think we should carry on as we are, for the time being,' she said coolly.

'I don't know if I can,' he murmured. 'The whole thing has backfired. I'll have to think it over and decide what to do.'

The day passed quickly. Mrs Jackson, middle-aged and motherly, appeared promptly at ten o'clock and tidied away the breakfast things while Rhiannon looked through the cupboards and wrote out a long shopping list.

'I'll give you a hand with your gear,' Shane offered, and together they began to unpack her boxes. He carried her clothes into the main bedroom and she hung them alongside his in the vast fitted wardrobe.

'Won't Mrs Jackson think it odd to make up two beds?' she asked, following him back into the spare room to collect more piles of clothes.

'There aren't two beds.'

'What do you mean? Where did you sleep?'

'Downstairs on the couch, and mighty uncomfortable it was too. It's about a foot shorter than I am,' he rubbed the small of his back and winced. 'I ache all over!'

'I'm sorry.' Her apology was automatic, then she remembered, with a flash of pique, that it was not *her* fault he had spent the night downstairs. 'We must order a second bed today.'

'Like hell!' he snapped. 'What would Mrs Jackson think if the first purchase we made on our honeymoon was a second bed? No, I'll just have to get used to the couch, that's all. We can buy a bed later when we start furnishing the whole house.'

'Kiss me,' Rhiannon demanded suddenly.

'No.' He stepped back, a strange expression on his face.

'Quick—a kiss,' she teased, standing on tiptoe before him, offering her lips. 'Mrs Jackson is coming upstairs, and you know we must act like newlyweds.'

Shane tilted his head to one side and listened. Sure enough, there were sounds of footsteps on the stairs.

'We have to pretend in public for the next twelve months,' Rhiannon pointed out, sliding her arms around his waist. His breathing was ragged, and she could feel the firm muscles quivering beneath the thin fabric of his shirt.

'You don't know what you're doing to me, you little vixen,' he muttered, before taking her savagely in his arms. 'Or perhaps you do.' His mouth was greedy, and

Rhiannon pressed herself against him, overjoyed at the knowledge that he was finding it almost impossible to control himself. Eventually he released her.

'I don't think I can go through with this,' he said, almost to himself, as he turned away. 'We're not pretending—you know it, and so do I.'

'Don't worry,' her tone was deliberately flippant. 'Let's go shopping!'

Before Shane left the house he put on his 'disguise'—the dark glasses and a denim cap—then they motored to the nearby town and began working their way down the shopping list. The 'disguise', combined with his newly trimmed hair, did the trick and he remained incognito, though his height and good looks drew several appreciative glances. They had a quick bite to eat at lunchtime, then spent the afternoon completing their purchases. Mrs Jackson had left when they returned, and Shane showed Rhiannon around the house in daylight. He was obviously delighted with his new home, which was set in an acre of ground, with wide lawns, and a fruit and vegetable garden to one side. The spacious grounds were filled with a neglected array of flowering bushes and trees, and spring flowers spilled haphazardly from flower beds on either side of the gravel drive at the front of the house.

'The garden is well stocked,' he said, 'but it needs some hard work—we must organise Mrs Jackson's son.'

'We could grow vegetables and freeze them,' Rhiannon smiled.

'Something else for the shopping list!'

'And we could have a greenhouse and grow our own flowers from seed.' She grabbed Shane's arm and squeezed it in her enthusiasm. 'Next time we go shopping I'll buy a gardening book and we can plan what we want to grow.'

'Don't forget we need the more mundane things, like spades,' Shane laughed.

'And we can start a compost heap,' Rhiannon continued, 'and buy some annuals, and perhaps a hanging basket of geraniums and lobelia in the front porch.'

He put his arm round her. 'Give us a chance, there's the house to furnish too!'

'And a time limit—twelve months,' she reminded him tightly, fracturing the lighthearted mood. His good humour faded like an eclipse of the sun, and he turned and walked away into the house. His sullen mood lasted for the rest of the day. Rhiannon was sorry she had introduced the sour note, but it had to be said. She knew she could derive immense pleasure from furnishing the house and tending to the garden, but it was foolish to forget that at the end of the year they would part and go their separate ways.

At ten o'clock she pleaded a tiredness she did not feel and went off to bed. She was in no mood to coax Shane into a good temper, though she had no doubt she could. She heard him moving around the house, but he never approached her door, and eventually the house was quiet, and she fell into a fitful sleep.

A sky of rich blue and a golden sun greeted her as she drew aside the heavy curtains the next morning, and when she opened the windows the air was fragrant with the smell of the heavy-blossomed lilac in the garden. She chose a sleeveless shift dress with a ruffled neckline in rustcoloured cotton, which emphasised the auburn gloss of her hair. When she opened the door of the lounge she was surprised to find Shane still asleep, although bright sunlight was pouring in through the uncurtained windows. He was lying on his back, one arm flung carelessly above his head, a white woollen blanket across his legs. His hair was tousled, and there was a dark shadow of stubble on his chin. He was peaceful, his restlessness eliminated. Quietly Rhiannon knelt beside him. She had never seen him asleep before, and she leant forward to touch a curl of thick hair on his forehead. He stirred, then sleepily opened his eyes and smiled. Her heart pounded. The surly mood of yesterday had vanished. Lazily he put his arm around her shoulders and drew her close. His skin was warm, with a sweet, altogether masculine smell.

'I want you, I want you,' he murmured drowsily, his
mouth brushing hers. He fumbled with the buttons on
her dress and for a moment Rhiannon held herself tense,
but then the movements of his hands began to awaken
warm sensations within her which were impossible to
deny, and she relaxed. Slowly he raised her to a pitch of
passion she had never imagined possible, and yet his
eyes were closed and he seemed to be half asleep as he
languorously stroked her silken skin and explored her
willing mouth. His breathing was deep and rhythmic,
and his body began to move impatiently as she rubbed
herself against him in response to the demands of his
fingers. She wondered, for a fleeting second, if he knew
which woman it was he was making love to.

'There's not enough room,' he muttered, stirring uncomfortably on the cramped couch.

'Let's go to bed,' she whispered, her pulses dizzy with
desire.

At her words Shane opened his eyes wide. 'No,' he
said clearly, suddenly wide awake and in complete control of himself, 'I refuse to take advantage of you.'

'You're not taking advantage,' Rhiannon cried desperately. 'I want you to make love to me.'

'Only because I've aroused you.' He pushed her aside
and stood up, pulling the blanket around him. 'I'm sorry
I did, but you were too tempting. I thought if I kept my
eyes closed that would make it all right, but of course it
doesn't! Just keep away from me, Rhiannon, *for both
our sakes*. I tricked you into marrying me, but I'm not
tricking you into sleeping with me.'

There was a sudden ring at the doorbell. 'Mrs
Jackson,' he announced with profound relief. 'Saved by
the bell!'

'You're despicable!' she flared, and ran away up the
stairs to her room. She lay face downwards on the bed,
the blood beating madly in her temples as she alternated
non-stop between hating Shane and desiring him. How
much simpler life would have been if Brad had lived,

and Shane had never had the opportunity to create this emotional havoc, she thought querulously. Gradually her distress became controllable and when she appeared for breakfast, a quarter of an hour later, she was composed. Only a hint of redness around her eyes indicated that her apparent calmness was an external veneer. Mrs Jackson quickly disappeared upstairs to make the bed and dust, and they were left alone.

'We need to go shopping again,' Rhiannon said frostily as she poured herself a second cup of coffee. 'If you want curtains and decorating done before the Far East tour then we should start gathering ideas and samples as soon as possible.'

'And we'll buy you a gardening book,' Shane added, his eyes watchful. She ignored his comment. She had decided that she was no longer interested in the garden, its time span was longer than twelve months, instead she would devote her energies to furnishing the house. Shane had given her a free hand and an open cheque book, and she knew it would be fun to furnish such an attractive house. Anything long-term, however, must be his responsibility. The telephone rang as they were finishing breakfast.

'That was the guy who will be soundproofing the music room,' Shane told her, coming back from the hall. 'He wants to come this morning. Do you mind going shopping alone? I ought to be here to explain exactly what I require.'

'I shall be perfectly happy by myself,' she assured him coldly. 'You don't mind me driving your car?'

'Not as long as you're careful.'

Rhiannon couldn't decide whether he was anxious about her or the expensive BMW!

He passed her the keys and a handful of notes as she gathered up her jacket. 'No wifely goodbye kiss?' he enquired, lifting one supercilious eyebrow as she passed by him to the front door. Rhiannon's eyes swam with hot tears and she hurried out to the car. He was merciless! He had raised her to a point of complete and utter surrender, and then pushed her aside, for a second time. She was determined it would not happen again.

'I hate you!' she blazed, flinging open the car door. Shane leant calmly against the stone porch, his long legs crossed at the ankle and his arms folded. There was the merest hint of uncertainty in his eyes as he watched the car cross his vision and disappear down the drive.

Rhiannon bought everything on her list, then lunched at a fast food restaurant. In the afternoon she visited several furniture shops, collecting brochures and discussing the suitability of fabrics. Decorating and furnishing the house from scratch was a major task, and she was determined to do it properly. It would take her mind off her emotional problems. She deliberately took her time and didn't hurry home, peevishly half hoping that her prolonged absence might worry Shane, for he deserved to be punished for his objectionable behaviour. It was early evening when she returned home, tired and footsore. As she climbed from the car she heard the sound of the piano through the open windows of the music room. Shane was totally absorbed, his left hand picking out notes, while the right one scribbled frantically on a sheet of paper.

He looked up in surprise when she walked through the door.

'Back already?'

Rhiannon gritted her teeth. She'd been gone most of the day and he appeared to have hardly missed her.

'Come here,' he instructed, moving to one side of the piano stool. Against her will she sat down beside him, acutely sensitive to the rub of his broad shoulder against hers. 'Listen to this, and tell me what you think.' He played her several bars and a haunting refrain filled the room.

'I like it,' she assured him as he finished playing, her annoyance beginning to seep away beneath his eagerness for her opinion.

'Honestly?'

'Honestly. I don't know much about music, but I

know what I like. What is it?'

'It might be a theme for that modern opera I'm going to write. I'm basing it on the life of Rasputin. There's a hell of an amount of research to be done, but the idea fascinates me. I will have to do some extensive reading and study the work of Russian composers, to give me a feel for the era. It's odd—I've been chewing it over in my mind for months, but today it suddenly gelled and I managed to write something down on paper. Of course, I might tear the whole thing up tomorrow morning, but at least it's a start.' His eyes shone with pleasure.

'Perhaps it's the house, perhaps it has the right vibrations,' suggested Rhiannon, watching leaves on the trees outside the window move in the soft evening breeze. 'Perhaps it stimulates you.'

'Or maybe it's you.' His voice was low. She shook her head and stood up, finding it impossible to sit beside him while the atmosphere was so charged with their mutual desire. Shane put out a hand as though to detain her, but then he thought better of it and closed the piano lid. 'Eddie phoned, he's asked me to meet some fellow they're auditioning. He isn't sure about his musical strength and needs my opinion. I don't want to go up to London, but I suppose it's the least I can do, considering it's my fault they need a replacement.' He cast her a wary glance. 'I told him we'd drive up tomorrow. We can stay overnight in a hotel and come back here the following morning.'

Rhiannon panicked. She didn't see how she could possible cope with sleeping, platonically, in the same room as Shane.

'I'll stay here,' she told him weakly. 'There are people coming from the interior decorators tomorrow, and a salesman is bringing a selection of curtain materials the next day.'

'Perhaps it would be for the best,' Shane agreed quickly. 'I'll try and work something out as regards you and me. I know it's late in the game, but I've discovered I do have principles too, you've not cornered the market.

Perhaps it would be for the best if I removed myself completely from your life; it seems the honourable thing to do.'

He waited for her answer, but Rhiannon said nothing; she didn't know what to say. Shane gave a grunt of impatience. 'Are you sure you'll be alright on your own?'

'Quite sure.'

He left early next morning, and she watched him go with a mixture of relief and despair. Everything had happened so quickly—the signed agreement, their marriage, and now his rejection. Their relationship was certainly built on tottering foundations, and with a sigh of resignation Rhiannon decided that it was a good thing it would all be over in a year's time and she could revert to a more placid existence. She went back into the house as the car disappeared and made another cup of coffee. There was nothing to be gained from brooding. Shane would make his own decisions; he always had. She picked up the shade cards and brochures, and spent the morning carefully walking around the house, working out which rooms enjoyed the most sun, which would suit a light, airy atmosphere, which should be cosy. When the interior decorator arrived he was delighted to discover a customer with a good sense of colour and a healthy bank balance, and the entire afternoon passed in deep discussion of colour schemes, fabrics and furniture. Rhiannon knew what she didn't want—an overcrowded chintzy look, but was eager for expert advice as to alternatives. When the man left her head was buzzing with a multitude of ideas, and as she went to bed she was still pondering over colour matches and furnishing styles.

The following day brought another long discussion, this time with the curtain salesman, and eventually Rhiannon chose an array of samples to show to Shane on his return. Although he had said he was perfectly happy with whatever she chose, she wanted his approval before she went ahead. It was *his* house, after all. She was still considering the various samples of curtain material, in conjunction with a book of wallpaper patterns, when the telephone rang in the late afternoon. Shane had spoken to her the previous evening to check that she was safe and now, she decided as she hurried to lift the receiver, he was probably ringing to tell her he was on his way home.

'Hello, Rhi. I saw Shane this afternoon and he suggested I give you a ring.' It was David. Her heart plummeted with disappointment. 'He was involved in a second session with that new fellow Eddie has discovered. I reckon the guy's too inexperienced, and Shane doesn't think much of him either.' David went off into a long, rambling tale about the young man and other possibles, then he wanted to hear all about the house. Rhiannon happily gave him a description of the rooms and the way she wanted to furnish them.

'How's Cheryl?' she asked, pausing for breath.

'Fine,' his reply was brief. 'By the way, Maxine's back in town. I bumped into her yesterday. She was furious to hear you and Shane are married.'

'I don't know why she should be,' Rhiannon retorted heatedly, suddenly on edge. Maxine was the last person she wanted to hear about. 'It was all over between them long ago.'

'That's not the way she tells it. She's still hot for him.'

'Well, she's out of luck,' Rhiannon snapped. 'He's a married man now.'

'And why should that make any difference?' David asked impudently, making her quake in trepidation. She was only too aware that her relationship with Shane was vulnerable, and Maxine was a determined young woman.

'We've only been married a few days, surely even Maxine would have the decency to wait a while before attempting to renew their affair?'

'I've no idea, but she'd be at him like a shot if she knew it was only a business agreement.' He paused. 'Or have you both decided otherwise?'

She could sense his leer. 'No, we haven't. It's a *platonic* agreement, and always will be.'

'Shane surprises me,' David said laconically. 'I presumed the whole idea of him marrying you was to get you into bed.'

After dinner Rhiannon lit the log fire, for the evening was cool, and settled down on the couch, her legs tucked beneath her. She was immersed in a paperback novel when the shrill noise of the telephone interrupted the quiet. She had been expecting Shane for the past two hours, but still he hadn't returned, and she was beginning to wonder if he had had trouble with the car.

'Good evening, Rhiannon,' he said formally, as though she were merely an acquaintance. 'I've been delayed. I was with Eddie and his hopeful, and we failed to realise how late it was. It's been a hell of a day, and I'm tired out. Would you mind if I stay over in London tonight? I don't fancy driving down now in the dark. I'll leave at the crack of drawn and be with you first thing in the morning.'

'That's fine,' she said smoothly, her fingers gripping the receiver so tightly that the blood drained away. 'See you tomorrow.'

Quickly she replaced the receiver before Shane could say anything else. She refused to listen to his lies. She knew why he had chosen to spend the night in London—he had met Maxine again.

CHAPTER FIVE

WITH a series of emphatic blasts on the car horn Shane returned home. True to his word, it was before nine in the morning, and Rhiannon was only half awake as she hurriedly climbed out of bed. She pulled on her negligee before running barefooted downstairs. She glanced at the clock and took grim satisfaction in the knowledge that he must have left Maxine in the dawn hours in order to arrive so early. She felt a stab of malicious pleasure at knowing that the model's beauty sleep must have been ruined. Shane was waiting on the doorstep, arms lazily folded, when she unbolted the front door.

'Hello, sleepyhead,' he grinned, noticing the smudged shadows beneath her eyes, and the untidy mane of chestnut hair. He reached out to caress her soft, flushed cheek, but Rhiannon moved away quickly. He sighed impatiently, and followed her through into the kitchen.

Rhiannon plugged in the percolator. 'Will you have some breakfast?'

'Yes, please.'

'Did you deal with everything which needed to be dealt with?' she asked, sawing at a loaf of bread with unnecessary vigour. If there was a double meaning to her words Shane didn't appear to notice.

'I had a productive time,' he assured her, putting the cups and saucers on the table. 'We've scrapped the fellow Eddie found, so the search continues. There are more auditions planned for later in the week. We worked out the programme for the London concert. Several numbers from the new album will be included, so I've made a start arranging them. We've chosen the next single and chewed over some ideas for a video. I also collected information on Rasputin, there's a pile of books in the car.'

'You've been busy.' Rhiannon kept a careful eye on the toast beneath the grill. 'David phoned—he said he'd met you. Did you see anyone else in town?' Her voice was carefully casual. She knew she was forcing the issue unnecessarily, half hoping, half fearing he would mention Maxine, but his reply was non-committal.

'No one special, just the usual crowd, a few guys from the band. They all appear to have had a great time at our wedding—that was the main topic of conversation. They send you their love.'

'Sounds as though you never had a moment's peace.' She pushed the tumbled hair from her brow and sat down at the table.

'I did manage to get away for a walk around a little churchyard near my old apartment—I always go there when I need to think. It's a tranquil spot, green and secluded, hidden away in the centre of the city and very conducive to thought. I wanted to work out what to do about us.'

She was hardly able to speak as sudden panic gripped her throat, 'Did you reach a decision?'

'No. *Don't push me, Rhi.*'

She hesitated, biting her lip, then said with false brightness, 'I've masses of fabric samples to show you. If you like the ones I've chosen we could drive into town and order the curtains, and perhaps arrange dates for the decorators to come in.'

'Not today. There's some whizz-kid reporter arriving early afternoon to interview us and take photographs.'

'That's short notice,' she protested tartly. 'I must go into the village and buy food for dinner, otherwise we shall starve, and if he's going to take photographs I'll have to try and brighten up the house, *and* I want to wash my hair. Why didn't you tell me before?'

'I would have told you last night,' Shane's tone was calm, 'but you slammed down the receiver so pretty damn quick I didn't have the chance.'

'I was tired, there was nothing else to say,' she waffled.

The cold flash of exasperation in his blue eyes indicated his disbelief.

'Why is a reporter coming so soon? We've only been married a few days, and the house is in no fit state to be photographed. Couldn't he wait until it's been decorated and properly furnished? The rooms are so bare now.'

'It's Eddie's bright idea,' Shane said patiently. 'He wants as much publicity as possible about us setting up home as newlyweds—he reckons it'll take the heat off me. He's still hoping I might change my mind and stay with Submission.' He raised a cynical brow. 'He was over the moon when this reporter asked for an interview, apparently it's supposed to be a privilege to fall under his scrutiny.' He snorted indignantly. 'His name is Buck Andrews.'

Rhiannon opened her eyes wide. 'I've heard of him, he's all the rage. He writes for a daily newspaper and in a leading women's magazine—he takes his own photographs too. His articles are outspoken. He's reputed to be extremely shrewd in getting down to the nitty-gritty of people's personalities, no holds barred. Once you've been written about by Buck Andrews, you know you've arrived.'

'Sounds the typical obnoxious journalist,' Shane said sarcastically. 'I dislike him already. If he imagines he's going to write an in-depth article full of frank confessions from you and me, then he's sadly mistaken. My God, I don't know how these fellows have the nerve to probe into other people's private lives! They're bloodsuckers!'

Rhiannon filled all the jugs she could find with garden flowers in an attempt to brighten the house. She did her shopping, then rushed back to shampoo her hair, catching it into a gleaming knot at the back of her head, with loose curls around her ears. She wore a brightly patterned Hawaiian-style shirt in vivid blues and greens, and a pair of avocado-coloured pants. She paid particular attention to her face, applying smoky blue shadow to her lids, and a touch of blusher to her high cheekbones. Amber lipstick emphasised her full mouth. She was determined to look her best if her photograph was to be circulated throughout the British Isles.

By two o'clock they were ready and waiting. Rhiannon sat nervously on the edge of the couch, while Shane prowled uneasily between the door and the window. He resembled a sleek panther, with his shiny black hair and light eyes, poised to attack at the slightest hint of danger. He was dressed in a navy towelling shirt edged with white at the collar, and navy slacks. At the sound of a car outside on the gravel he caught hold of her hand. 'Newlyweds, very much in love, don't forget,' he snapped fiercely. 'We can't afford to have this guy suspect anything is less than normal.' A nerve throbbed in his cheek.

'Calm down!' Rhiannon deposited a casual kiss on his cheek, and he smiled thinly.

'Sorry, I'm overreacting, but if this guy is as shrewd as he's reputed to be, we could end up in difficulties. I've always hated interviews, I shall be damned glad when it's finished.'

There was a fanfare on the doorbell.

'Kiss me,' Shane demanded. Rhiannon was surprised by the emotion in his voice, but after a moment's hesitation lifted her mouth to his. He kissed her deeply, holding her close, as though taking strength from her. Instinctively she slipped two fingers between the buttons of his shirt and caressed the dark hair beneath. He moved impatiently.

'I'm just keeping my part of the bargain,' she assured him solemnly, noting the race of confused emotions which crossed his face. She was well aware that a prominent magazine article emphasising how besotted she and Shane were with each other would attract Maxine's attention. It was high time she was taught a lesson—not to meddle with other people's husbands, whatever the circumstances.

Rhiannon nearly laughed out loud when she saw Buck

Andrews. In shiny black leather trousers and a sleeveless black satin tee-shirt with an obscene slogan, he looked far more like a pop star than Shane. He was in his mid-twenties, with bleached platinum hair, cut short and spiky on top. He was only a little taller than she was, around five foot nine, and his thickset body was hung with a vast array of cameras and light meters. He sported a splendid display of exotic, and erotic, tattoos on his muscular arms, and wore two heavy gold chains around his neck. He positively pulsated with vitality.

'Hi there, mates,' he greeted them in a cheery Cockney accent. He beamed at Rhiannon and gave a long, low insolent whistle. 'You're a bit of all right,' he said, looking her up and down with exaggerated lasciviousness. 'When your old man gets tired of you, give me a call.' He winked lewdly, making Rhiannon laugh. He was just too extreme to be taken seriously.

'I shan't get tired of her,' Shane assured him, pulling her possessively close and kissing her brow.

There was an immediate prickle of antagonism between the two men, and as they walked around the house and garden, and Buck plied his questions, the tense atmosphere grew. Despite his outrageous appearance and often impudent probing, Rhiannon couldn't help liking him, though it was soon obvious Shane felt otherwise. She found Buck's cheeky personality fun, and he chattered away happily, non-stop, seemingly oblivious of Shane's reserve. Every so often he would scribble something in a notebook, while Shane watched warily. It was a relief when the reporter asked about plans for their new home, and Shane relaxed sufficiently to enthuse about the house and its history. He was also willing to discuss his musical background, and his plans for widening his musical range in the future. He made no mention of his anticipated departure from Submission. News of the change in the group's line-up would only be announced when a new member had been signed. Eddie had asked them both to be discreet. Premature speculation on Shane's withdrawal would lead only to increased interest from the press, which they all wanted to avoid.

'Why the hasty marriage?' Buck asked offhandedly as they returned to the lounge. Rhiannon poured out glasses of white wine and handed them round as she waited for Shane's reaction. He frowned. Buck's eyes were calculating, sharp as razors, and the two men sized each other up like duellists. The interview suddenly changed into an interrogation. 'There was no hint of a romance between you. As far as I can discover you never dated.'

'You don't know all the facts.' Shane viewed him with cold distaste. 'I've loved Rhiannon for ages, but I had a hell of a job persuading her to marry me.' He was obviously disconcerted, and Rhiannon leant forward and kissed him in a sudden spontaneous desire to comfort him. His lips were warm and sweet from the wine. Buck watched them keenly.

'I still don't understand. Why the on-the-spot decision to marry? Was it for a purpose?'

'I'm not pregnant, if that's what you think!' burst out Rhiannon hotly, her face bright pink. Both men laughed out loud at the note of righteous indignation in her voice, and for a moment the taut atmosphere slackened.

'I'm sure all your fans would like to know if you have a vigorous love life,' Buck said slyly.

'Mind your own business,' Rhiannon told him firmly, and Shane shot her a grateful glance.

'How about revealing whether Shane is as raunchy as he looks?'

'Raunchy?' Shane savoured the word, an amused smile tugging at the corner of his mouth. 'My God, is that what I'm supposed to be?'

'Tell me what you both wear in bed—anything or nothing?' insisted Buck. Shane's amusement disappeared instantly, to be replaced by anger which filled the room like shock waves.

'Okay, okay,' Buck grinned unashamedly, 'I retract that, but frankly it's the kind of information the public wants about sex symbols. Now, how about some intimate photographs? I've taken plenty of the pair of you in the garden, but I need some close-ups of Rhiannon. She's a beautiful girl. She could end up with a fan club of her own after my article.'

'No.' Shane stood up abruptly. 'Nothing close. I don't want her to be recognised in public. It's bad enough me being stared at continuously—I don't want Rhiannon to be plagued.'

'Be reasonable! How do you expect me to illustrate the article without any close-ups?'

Shane clenched his fists and glared down menacingly, making no attempt to conceal his dislike of the reporter. *No close-ups of Rhiannon,*' he ground out. 'Get this straight, Andrews, you're only here to write an article for some trashy magazine because my manager reckons it's a good idea. I know damn well that my name on the front cover will boost circulation, *so I'm doing you a favour.* I don't give a toss about publicity myself, and I have no wish for details of my prowess as a lover and other juicy snippets to be splashed over the pages. I also refuse to allow my wife to become a celebrity by association.'

There was a fraught silence. Buck fiddled with one of his cameras and waited.

'How about a profile close-up, or some shot that isn't too distinct?' Rhiannon compromised, slipping her arm around Shane's waist as she tried to lighten the atmosphere. He gave a heavy sigh.

'I could angle it so that Rhiannon isn't too recognisable,' Buck said quickly, taking advantage of Shane's deliberation.

'Okay,' he agreed heavily. 'But I want to see all the prints before they appear. Where do you want to photograph us?'

Buck's natural audacity bounced back. 'How about the bedroom?'

'It's not furnished,' Shane said crossly. 'It's almost empty, like the rest of the house.'

'I presume you have a bed? I could take you frolicking amongst the sheets, that would delight your fans.'

'There's no bloody way you're photographing us in bed,' Shane growled.

'O.K., mate, just joking. I'm not looking for trouble. All I'm asking for is a little co-operation. Let's move around the house and I'll take shots of you both in the different rooms, that suit?'

Buck knew exactly what he required on film. He was quick, easy and professional, and Rhiannon's initial embarrassment at being photographed began to disappear beneath his lighthearted banter. She started to enjoy herself, and even Shane relaxed a little.

'Sexy cuddle—housewifely peck—deep gaze into each other's eyes—passionate embrace—soulful look into middle distance——' Buck issued a steady stream of instructions like a sergeant-major, until eventually Rhiannon burst out laughing. She leant against Shane, her hands clasped behind his neck, her body convulsed with giggling.

'*I want you so much,*' Shane whispered hoarsely into her ear. He kissed her again, and his hands moved urgently from her shoulderblades down to her waist, and then to her hips, pressing her hard against his thighs and leaving her in no doubt that he was sexually aroused.

'Right—that's it, then,' Buck called, snapping a final couple of shots. 'I've taken enough film. I'll arrange for prints to be delivered to your London office as soon as possible.'

Shane released Rhiannon to frown across at the reporter. 'See that you do,' he ordered.

'How about a follow-up spread in a few months' time?' Buck suggested as they walked outside to his sports car. 'Rhiannon could reveal all on what it's like being married to a member of Submission.'

She hesitated, biting her lip. The idea had its advantages, it would emphasise to the fans, and to Maxine, that Shane was firmly married. Then she felt a dull ache in the pit of her stomach as she realised they might be distinctly *un*married in a few months' time if Shane decided it was better for them to part.

'*No!*' Shane thundered, and she wondered if he, too, was thinking along the same lines.

'It's a good idea, isn't it, Rhiannon?' Buck appealed, opening the car door. Perhaps it did make sense, she thought, and pursed her lips.

'*No*,' Shane repeated loudly.

Buck ignored him. 'I'll come and see you again, when this monster of yours isn't around,' he winked at Rhiannon, 'and then we can share a tête-à-tête.' He slipped into the low driving seat, and blew her a kiss as he drove gaily away down the drive.

Shane's eyes were like ice chips. 'I was right,' he strode quickly back into the house, 'he *was* obnoxious, asking prying questions and flirting with you the entire afternoon. I don't know why you encouraged him.' He flung her an angry look.

'I didn't encourage him,' she protested. 'He was good fun.'

'Good fun! He made it pretty obvious *he'd* like to be the one frolicking amongst the sheets with you.'

'So what's wrong with that?' she flared, the Welsh accent lifting her words. 'He'd no doubt make love to me properly, instead of leaving me up in the air.' Her pent-up feelings of resentment and frustration welled to the surface. 'He wouldn't go sneaking off to London to meet another girl!'

'What do you mean?'

'You refuse to make love to me,' she gulped, her eyes suspiciously bright, 'but you make love to Maxine. That's why you spent last night in London.'

'*You're wrong!*'

'You didn't see Maxine?'

'Yes, I did,' he scowled, rubbing the back of his neck in agitation, 'but I didn't sleep with her.'

'Why not—surely having a wife wouldn't stop you? And don't forget I shall be gone in twelve months' time,' she taunted.

A dull red flush flooded Shane's face. He took a step towards her, and for an instant she thought he was going to strike her.

'It did stop me,' he said flatly. 'I admit I entertained the foolish idea that if I made love to her perhaps it would give me a measure of relief and clear you out of my system. I thought I'd be able to see the situation more clearly then, instead of being in this bloody emotional state of not knowing what to do. But it didn't work like that. We had a drink together, but I couldn't keep my mind on what she was saying, I was too busy thinking about you. As soon as I could, I said goodbye and returned to the hotel—*alone*. I don't give a damn about her. I want you.'

'Even though I'm a virgin?' She gave a small, bitter laugh. 'That's one thing you can't accuse Maxine of being.'

'Don't be vulgar, it doesn't suit you.'

'But what suits *you*?' she demanded, perilously close to tears.

'I don't know.' His voice was thick and uneven. He reached out and put his hand on her shoulder, but Rhiannon turned away, tears spilling down her cheeks. 'Just leave me alone,' she fiercely shook off his hand, 'I don't want anything more to do with you!'

'You can't mean that.'

'I do, I do!' she cried. She flung herself from the room and ran upstairs, blinded by hot, salty tears. She threw herself on to the bed, sobbing wildly in rage and misery. In the distance she heard the slam of the front door and the revving of the car engine. Shane had gone.

The evening seemed endless. Rhiannon sat before the blazing log fire miserably trying to read her book, but the words made no sense. Her mind buzzed with unanswered and unanswerable questions. Where had Shane gone? Perhaps this time he would go to Maxine and make love to her? Would he return home, and, more important, did she want him to return? Surely it made more sense if they separated now? After all, everything would end in twelve months' time, what was the point of them tearing each other apart as they were doing now? The whole marriage was a fiasco. They were too emotionally involved to continue in the present state of affairs, something had to change. She sat alone, unhappily going over the situation time and again, without reaching any conclusion. By midnight Shane had not returned, and she decided, morosely, he had driven up to London, and Maxine.

She went to bed, and eventually drifted off to sleep, only to be woken by a vague noise. She rubbed her eyes in the darkness and peered sleepily at the luminous dial of the clock. It was after two. She remembered, with an uneasy shudder, that she had forgotten to bolt the front door. She would feel happier if it was secure, so she crept downstairs and was stood on tiptoe, pushing home the top bolt, when the lounge door opened.

'Here, let me help.'

She jumped violently at the sound of his voice, her heart thumping wildly. 'Shane! I didn't know you were back.'

He was fully dressed, his tan leather jacket over his shirt and slacks. He reached up and easily shot the bolt. 'I've been home about an hour—I hope I didn't disturb you,' he said anxiously, as they went together into the lounge. 'I've been sitting in the dark, looking into the embers of the fire.' He switched on the table lamp. 'For heaven's sake, *cover yourself up*.' His eyes were drawn magnetically to her sleep-soft body in the coffee-coloured nightgown. He removed his jacket and draped it around her shoulders. 'How do you expect me to stay in one piece when you're tantalising me like that?' he asked raggedly. Rhiannon pulled the jacket about her and sat down beside him on the couch. She was too sleepy to argue, or rationalise her feelings. There was a bottle of whisky and a glass on the carpet.

'I've been drinking,' he said, noticing her glance, 'but I'm not drunk.'

'Where have you been?'

'I drove around for a while and had some dinner. Then I bought a bottle of whisky at an off-licence and drove down to the coast. I had a few swigs in the car, and had a long walk along the shore.'

'I'm glad you came home. I didn't really mean what I said this afternoon. I guess we're both uptight at the moment.'

Shane nodded, a rueful smile twisting one corner of his mouth. Without thinking Rhiannon reached across and touched his cheek with the back of her fingers. Shane took hold of her hand and kissed it, his eyes dark with yearning. She moved her shoulders and the leather jacket dropped behind her. Wordlessly he took her in his arms. His breath was warm and his mouth tasted of whisky. As the blood began to flow hotly beneath the surface of her skin Rhiannon traced a pattern in the thick ebony curls around his ears.

'There's only one place for me,' he said at last, as though reaching a difficult decision, 'and that's in your bed. I can't fight it any longer, I can't resist you.' He gathered her in his arms and carried her up the stairs, where he laid her gently on the bed. She reached out for him as he threw off his clothes, her lips on his face, his shoulders, his chest. Her hands explored the firm, golden-skinned muscles of his body. He slipped the nightgown easily over her head and tossed it aside. Then he was with her, holding her close as though he would never let her go. His mouth was on hers, demanding, taking, giving. His fingertips caressed her silken skin, teasing the proud nipples, making her body move with the erotic rhythm of love until she moaned aloud with desire. Wild music filled her ears. She caught at the thick black hair on his head, twisting it around her fingers as their bodies moved together, searching and finding, then Shane took her. She gasped at a sharp stab of pain, then he relentlessly forced her upwards to a crest of ecstasy she had never known before. Her body convulsed, joining with his in a joyous release, before he carried

her down, down, down, with him on to the sweet, wonderful shore of fulfilment.

'My love, my love,' he murmured into her hair as
they lay together, drenched in sweat, exhausted by their
lovemaking. Later she cried, her tears trickling onto his
shoulder. 'I didn't hurt you, did I?' he asked anxiously,
holding her safe and close.

Rhiannon smiled through her tears and shook her
head. 'I'm crying because it was so wonderful—*you're*
so wonderful,' she tried to explain. Shane understood,
and held her until she drifted into a deep, contented
sleep. Later in the night she felt his lips on her throat,
his hands caressing her body until she ached with the
need of him. She gave herself to him once again in sweet
surrender and when, in the depths of desire, he cried
out that he loved her, she sighed softly to herself in the
darkness.

The sunlight was dazzling behind the curtains next
morning when Shane stirred beside her. 'That's Mrs
Jackson,' he said. Rhiannon rubbed her eyes, struggling
to break the blindfold of sleep. The doorbell was ringing.
He climbed out of bed and pulled on his dressing gown.
'I'll go and open the door.' As he padded downstairs
she stretched lazily, and gave a deep, satisfied sigh.
For the moment life was perfect, and she wouldn't spoil
it by wondering about the future. She was surprised
when Shane returned and slid back into bed beside her.

'Shouldn't we get up? Mrs Jackson will wonder what
we're doing.'

He gave a chuckle of pure delight. 'Don't be naïve,
Rhi. We're on our honeymoon, remember? She won't
be wondering what we're doing, *she'll know*. There's a
lot of wasted time to make up, and I fully intend making
love to you morning, noon and night.' His voice
deepened with his need of her. Slowly, sensually, he
dragged a long finger down across the high cheekbone,
her jaw and throat, her breast, her flat stomach, and on
and on. Rhiannon wriggled up against him as his
breathing quickened and his mouth opened on hers. She

had never known such an exquisite physical awareness before. Her mind stopped functioning, and her whole world was controlled by Shane's touch as her body responded—rising and falling, swelling and tightening.

'Thank God,' he breathed afterwards, as they lay together tired and sated. She fingered the damp hair on his chest and looked at him questioningly. 'I couldn't have pretended to pretend for much longer,' he explained. 'Every time you touched me you nearly drove me wild. I felt such a swine. I knew the correct thing was to go away, get out of your life and allow you to do things your own way, but I couldn't. I was in an emotional knot. I couldn't break it—the more I struggled, the tighter it became. Still,' he smiled, 'Now you're mine—properly.'

'Yes, I am,' she acknowledged happily, and she knew she was falling in love with him.

Rhiannon had never felt so vital and cherished in the whole of her life. The days were now full of love and laughter, and at times she thought she would die from a surfeit of happiness. Shane was a devoted and vigorous husband, and they spent long, joyful days together, furnishing the house, working in the garden, and making love. All they needed was each other, and she almost forgot they had agreed to separate after a year, for Shane never, ever, referred to it. They resented the days when his presence was required in London for recording sessions and meetings. On these occasions Rhiannon accompanied him, and lent a hand at the office. She enjoyed keeping in touch with the affairs of Submission and chatting with the other secretaries. Eddie was smugly delighted with the success of their marriage.

'I don't like to crow,' he said, ushering Rhiannon into his office for a private chat, 'but I will. Didn't I say you and Shane were right for each other?'

He looked so pleased with himself that she burst out laughing. 'I admit it, you're a clever fellow,' and she spread her hands in a gesture of satisfied defeat.

'And what a difference in Shane!' Eddie continued. 'I don't know what you're doing to him, but he's learning how to take life calmly. He doesn't snap at people's throats any longer. Even his restlessness has gone. Mind you, he's not been exposed to the fans for a while, he always was happier out of the limelight. Perhaps he'll start getting edgy again when rehearsals start for the London concert.' He searched through a heap of papers on his desk and produced a magazine. 'The Buck Andrews interview was very astute, wasn't it? Reading between the lines it's obvious he considers Shane is far more talented than the run-of-the-mill pop musician, and needs to stretch himself.'

'It's a good piece,' Rhiannon agreed. 'Sufficient claptrap to keep the fans contented, but also an intelligent profile on Shane. Buck's a smart man—despite his gimmicky appearance, he really penetrated the heart of Shane's problems.'

'Is he still writing that opera?'

'Off and on. He doesn't have much spare time. As you know, he's been working on the new arrangements, and we're also in the middle of decorating and furnishing the house.'

'Couldn't you persuade him to change his mind and stay with Submission? We're still auditioning, but we've not had any luck. He's a difficult man to follow.'

'He'll leave at the end of the agreement,' Rhiannon said firmly. 'Don't harbour any illusions, he won't change his mind.'

When she left the office she hailed a taxi and went to meet Anne for lunch. Shane, David and Tony were busily recording the first tracks of the new album and would be at work until the last possible moment before embarking on a mad scramble across London to the television studios where they were due to appear on an early evening pop music extravaganza. Afterwards she and Shane would return home, though he was due back in London two days later for rehearsals prior to the concert.

It was fun to see Anne again and catch up on all the news. They chattered happily all through lunch, and as Anne returned to work in the early afternoon it was with a firm promise that they would meet again soon. Rhiannon waved goodbye and took a lengthy shopping list from her handbag. When she had been a single girl and lived in the capital she had spent many happy hours looking around the shops, but then she had only been interested in clothes. Nowadays such matter-of-fact items as shower curtains and food mixers seemed far more appealing, and she turned an uninterested eye on the fashionable boutiques and resolutely made her way to the household department of Harrods.

By eight o'clock that evening she was footsore but content. She waited in the vestibule of the television studios with a faint smile on her face as she mentally ticked off her list of successful purchases. The car boot was crammed with a variety of domestic goods, and she could hardly wait to show them all to Shane. She glanced impatiently at the large clock on the wall. The show was scheduled to finish at eight, so in a few minutes' time he would be out to greet her and then they could motor home to Sussex. She happily wriggled her tired toes in her white strappy sandals and stretched. A young actor who was crossing the wide black and white tiled reception area slowed his stride to have a better look at her trim figure in the white suede skirt with its soft blouson top. Rhiannon gave him a vague smile and turned away to search, head down, in her leather handbag, for a hairbrush. Suddenly she became aware of someone standing before her. She was under scrutiny. As she glanced up her eyes widened in surprise. It was Maxine! Rhiannon felt a tremor of unease snake its way along her spine. The model was flamboyant in tight, shiny black elasticated trousers and a crimson blouse with huge, floppy sleeves, caught tight at the wrists. The blouse was unbuttoned beyond all realms of modesty, and a golden nugget swung provocatively in the cleavage. A curtain of dead straight ash-blond hair covered one eye as she stood, hands on shapely hips, looking down disdainfully. With a careless gesture she flicked the hair aside.

'Do you mind if I join you?' she asked serenely, sitting down on the low leather couch without bothering to wait for a reply. Rhiannon began brushing her hair with rapid strokes. Her throat was dry and her stomach muscles knotted with an irrational fear. She had heard no direct news of Maxine in the past weeks, though there was sufficient footage in the gossip columns to reveal that she was alive and well, and still fraternising with aristocratic playboys and celebrities.

'What are you doing here?' Rhiannon's seeming casual enquiry masked an inward whirlwind of agitation. She twisted her hair into a thick pleat and secured it with gold pins at the side of her head.

'I came to see Submission, of course,' Maxine purred, her wide mouth glistening with bright, moist lipstick. 'As you know, I'm very close to . . .' she paused suggestively, a gesture which was not lost on Rhiannon, 'the guys,' she concluded with a smug smile. She idly examined a magenta-painted talon. 'I was surprised to hear you and Shane have settled down to domesticity. Shane doesn't often care for long liaisons—unless, of course, it's someone special. He prefers to keep moving.'

The sheer maliciousness of the words took Rhiannon's breath away and she flushed. 'Obviously I must be that someone special,' she retorted frostily, replacing the brush in her handbag.

Maxine twitched her slender shoulders in a negative dismissal. 'The last time Shane and I were together,' she continued, casually rotating a delicate ankle, 'I told him your marriage hadn't a cat in hell's chance of succeeding.'

'And what did he say?' Rhiannon demanded hotly, her Welsh temper beginning to spark.

'He said he'd give it twelve months and see what happened then. It hardly sounded as though he considered it a long-term proposition. I had the distinct impression your days were numbered.'

Rhiannon didn't know what to say, and sat uncomfortably mute with misery as her subconscious fears were suddenly given astonishing clarity.

'Shane and I never really split up,' Maxine continued, with a pleased glance at the other girl's discomposure. 'We parted for a while, but the eternal *je ne sais quoi* still exists between us. If I hadn't disappeared to the States doubtless he wouldn't have become bored and . . .' She waved a manicured hand in the air which spoke a thousand words, and Rhiannon was filled with a desperate urge to bite it—*hard*. She was struggling to think of some clever, cutting reply, totally without success, when a straggle of people came into the vestibule. She looked up eagerly as Shane approached, and he gave her a quick smile before turning to Maxine.

'What are you doing here?' he asked sharply.

The model stood up gracefully, thrusting out her half naked breasts in a deliberately provocative manner. In her spindly black leather heels she could almost look Shane straight in the eye. 'Darling, I was at the studios auditioning for a little acting job when I realised Submission were here, so I thought I'd wait around and see you again.' She trailed an intimate finger across his jaw. 'I've missed you, we must get together again some time.' Her low voice throbbed with the promise of future delights.

Shane rebuffed her finger with a brisk movement of his dark head. 'And did you land the acting job?' he asked politely. The model rested her hand on his arm and launched into a highly coloured tale of her audition.

Rhiannon perched on the low sofa and looked up at the two of them, towering above her like magnificent Amazons. She fervently wished she was tall, like Maxine, but even in her highest heels she only reached Shane's chin. She felt at a distinct disadvantage, crouched at their feet, but was paralysed with despair,

incapable of standing as she remembered Maxine's
words. As she listened to Maxine's racy conversation
she began to feel like a country bumpkin. The thought
of her purchases in the car, which only a few minutes
ago had filled her with delight, made her squirm. Now
they seemed so ordinary. She could hardly break into
the conversation, which dripped with famous names and
fascinating innuendoes, with a reference to the unusual
shade of the dining room curtains. She stared at Shane,
willing him to sit down beside her, but instead he thrust
a nonchalant hand into his trouser pocket and eyed
Maxine up and down thoughtfully. And she was quite
an eyeful!

'Shane, come and join the others for photographs.'
Eddie hurried towards them, and Rhiannon stood up
quickly, grateful to be released from her torpor.

Shane's face clouded.

'It won't take long,' Eddie continued. 'The T.V. boys
want some publicity shots.'

Maxine moved languidly aside to chat with some
producer, and Shane took hold of Rhiannon's elbow,
and with ill-concealed reluctance allowed Eddie to usher
them forward into a corner of the reception area.
Rhiannon waited beside Eddie as Submission posed,
then noticed Maxine sashay over to speak to one of the
cameramen. It was an open secret that she was publicity-
crazy, but surely she wasn't so brazen as to try and
wheedle her way into a photograph with the group?
Rhiannon bit her lip, remembering times in the past
when photographs of Shane and Maxine together had
appeared in the newspapers.

'Can we take Shane and his new missus?' suggested
one of the cameramen, and Eddie pushed Rhiannon
forward to join Shane.

'I don't want you photographed,' Shane bit out
angrily, but it was too late, the cameras had already
started clicking. Shane sighed. 'I hate being photographed,' he grumbled, keeping his voice low so that
only Rhiannon could hear him. 'You've no idea how

pleased I shall be when the contract is ended and I can leave Submission. It can't come quickly enough. I'm longing to be free.'

'Touch of snogging, please,' yelled a photographer. Shane put his arm stiffly around Rhiannon, his jaw set in a taut line, but he reluctantly conceded defeat and kissed her briefly, his eyes warily assessing the audience. In the background Maxine gave a smothered giggle, and Rhiannon squirmed. So Maxine was amused by Shane's chaste kiss, was she! Rhiannon reached up and put her hands on either side of his face, pulling his mouth down to meet hers. She opened her lips and pressed them against his until he began to respond. His breathing quickened, and she slid her arms around his neck, thrusting her body against him in an open display of desire. Shane moved his mouth from hers. 'You're arousing me like mad,' he whispered hotly into her ear, and kissed her again. The cameras stopped clicking, and the photographers began to disperse. Rhiannon pushed herself away from Shane and turned to walk away, but he restrained her.

'What the hell are you playing at?' he asked with a puzzled flicker of amusement in his eyes.

'Nothing,' she answered pertly, with a toss of her head. 'Let's go home.' She started to walk ahead of him towards the glass swing doors.

'I can't.'

She stopped in her tracks.

'I'm sorry,' Shane explained, 'but I have to stay on. Eddie's signed up a replacement for me at long last, someone called Peter Willans. He wants him on stage at the concert, so I'll have to brief him. Also we've hit a few snags with the album which need ironing out. I'll have to stay in London until after the concert.'

From the corner of her eye Rhiannon caught a glimpse of black and flashing crimson as Maxine strolled by.

'See you soon, Shane,' she murmured throatily as she disappeared outside. Rhiannon rapidly put two and two together. It didn't take much imagination to work out why Shane's presence was suddenly vital in London. The domestic scene was beginning to bore him, he was moving on to more exciting pastures. Her senses reeled; what a fool she'd been!

'Why don't you stay on with me until after the concert?' Shane was asking, but it seemed to her a lukewarm suggestion at best.

'What's the point?' her voice was tart. 'With you at the recording studios or rehearsing all day long I'd only be hanging around. I'd rather go home and supervise the decorating.'

'You're right,' he agreed smoothly. 'But I shall miss you.'

He walked with her out to the car park and waited until she was safely settled in the driving seat of the BMW.

'I hate us being apart,' he complained, bending down to kiss her through the open window. 'Drive carefully, I'll ring you tomorrow. We'll meet at the concert, and then I promise we really will go home together.'

Rhiannon coolly returned his kiss. Then she switched on the ignition, and the luxury saloon slid forward. She sighed tremulously as Shane's image disappeared from the rear view mirror and she swung out on to the road. Through a mixture of blindness and optimism she had allowed herself to believe that their marriage was a proper one. How naïve she had been! Shane was only hers because of a business arrangement, and then only for twelve months, and he had already said he wished the arrangement was ended and he could be free. She remembered, too late, how he always refused to discuss the future, brushing it aside with some easy, joking comment. She had imagined he was content, but obviously the germ of restlessness was still within him. He had spent all his life on the move, from country to country, from girl to girl; why should he stop now? He was ruthless when it came to getting what he wanted. He had, by his own admission, forced her to marry him—there was nothing to stop him leaving her just as selfishly.

She chewed her lip, her body aching with unhappiness as she drove through the suburbs. She had coasted happily along, like a child who has been told everything is all right, presuming that their newly found love had changed everything, but now she doubted it. Very much indeed.

CHAPTER SIX

WHEN the decorators arrived early the next morning Rhiannon had already breakfasted. She had been lying awake since dawn, trying to make sense of the situation in which she found herself, and had risen before seven. She had washed her face and left it free from make-up. She pulled her hair back into two bunches before putting on a loose-fitting, rose-coloured velour jump suit. She was in no mood to make an effort with her appearance. She had pondered long and hard about Shane's feelings for her, and wondered briefly if she might wind up lost and frantic at the end of their marriage, while he moved smoothly on to a fresh location, a fresh woman. Slowly her spirits revived as she went through the automatic motions of washing up and changing the flowers, but her interest in the house now seemed only a diversion, her former enthusiasm had drained away.

Mrs Jackson came in at ten and made a fresh pot of tea for everyone, which she served with slices of moist banana cake which she had brought from home. Rhiannon was grateful for her company, and listened, as she sipped her tea, to Mrs Jackson prattling on about the progress of the painters, the arrival of new furniture, and Alan's hard work in the garden.

'Let's do a grand tour,' Rhiannon suggested, when they had washed up the tea cups, and together they walked through the house, while Mrs Jackson marvelled and enthused over the progress made. Despite her newly acquired disillusion Rhiannon felt a glow of pleasure. Her careful planning was beginning to pay dividends, and already there was an atmosphere of comfort and elegance. The house was bright and airy, with fresh, leafy plants spilling from white ceramic tubs, and curtains billowing softly in the breeze from the open windows. The basic colour scheme for the ground floor was muted shades of green, gold and off-white, but she had provided vivid touches of contrasting colour in a display of turquoise Venetian glass, Thai silk cushions in acid yellow and caramel, a collection of silver and bronze etchings, shelves full of multi-coloured books. It was a home which was pleasing to the eye, and yet functional and cosy.

I don't want to leave in a few months' time, she thought, gazing round. I've created this lovely home, part of me belongs here. She frowned as a sudden vision of Maxine stretched out on the pale green velvet sofa flashed through her mind, and swallowed hard. It was foolish to torment herself; the house did not belong to her, nor did Shane. He had made no move to include her in his future. It was time she faced up to reality.

The doorbell rang as she was watering the plants on the patio.

'Buck Andrews!' she exclaimed in surprise.

'The one and only,' he grinned, hands on hips as he surveyed her from head to toe. 'You're still as gorgeous as ever, even with a shiny face and flat shoes. The schoolgirl look suits you.'

'Flatterer!' she laughed, but his words were cheering, and she began to perk up. 'Come on in.'

Buck stepped before her into the house. He cut a spectacular figure, in silver-grey tight trousers and a silver lamé shirt. His hair now sported a silver streak among the platinum.

'Come into the kitchen, the painters are busy in the lounge,' Rhiannon explained, leading the way. Mrs Jackson's mouth gaped open as Buck bounced in.

'Hello, charmer,' he grinned. She gave a wary smile and retreated hastily to hang out the washing.

'I was down in Sussex, so I thought I'd drop by and see if I could persuade you to go ahead with a second article. The first one was well received.'

'It was good,' Rhiannon smiled. 'Can I get you a cup of coffee?'

'Please.' Buck sniffed. 'Did your monster approve of what I wrote?'

'Yes.'

'Yes, yes, or yes, maybe?'

'Yes, maybe,' she admitted. 'Shane resents having his private life written up for everyone to read.'

'It's all good publicity, keeps the pound notes rolling in,' he reminded her smoothly. 'Where's Shane now?'

Rhiannon surveyed him keenly, her head on one side. 'You know darn well where he is, Buck, I'm sure you must have checked. I don't believe for one moment you dropped by casually, you're much too busy for that.'

He grinned widely. 'You're right.' He rubbed his hands together in a parody of an old-fashioned villain. 'I wanted to be alone with you, my pretty little damsel.'

'Well, I'm alone, apart from Mrs Jackson and the painters, but don't imagine my defences will be non-existent because Shane isn't around to protect me. I have no intention of succumbing to your wily ways.'

Buck grinned. 'If you can keep your monster under control, I'm sure you'll have no difficulty with me! Be honest, how come you've kept Shane on the straight and narrow for—what is it—three months? He used to be a great lad for quick changes.'

'Good food and good lovin',' she quipped with imitation humour as she poured out his coffee. Her heart fluttered wildly at his words. Buck might be good company and easy to respond to, but she must never forget he was a member of the press. He didn't chat her up because he wanted to be her friend, the only thing he wanted from her was good copy.

'Can I quote you on that?' he asked quickly.

'No.' Her tone was curt.

Buck watched her warily for a moment, and then changed his tactics. 'Why has Eddie Beagle signed up a new guy? Are they going to change the format of Submission? I've heard strong rumours Shane wants to quit.' He sipped his coffee, watching her like a hawk over the brim of the cup.

'You're not playing fair,' she protested. 'I expect there'll be an announcement soon, but anything on group policy must come from Eddie, you know that.'

'Are there going to be changes?'

'I know nothing.'

He laughed in disbelief. 'There's something funny going on. I can't put my finger on it yet, but I will, and you're involved somewhere.'

Rhiannon shrugged.

'Maxine Daniels reckons your marriage won't last,' Buck said flippantly. 'She gives it a year at the most.'

Colour flooded Rhiannon's face. 'I think you'd better leave.' She stood up, pushing back her chair abruptly. 'Being a journalist doesn't give you carte blanche to intrude into my home and hope to cause trouble by repeating bitchy remarks. You are perfectly aware that Maxine is publicity-crazy. She'd say and do almost anything to get a mention in the newspapers.' Rhiannon's breathing was sharp, fast and audible.

'Cool it,' he waved a dismissive hand. 'Forget I said anything.' He sidestepped verbally. 'Have you met the new guy, Peter Willans?'

Rhiannon slumped back into her chair. Buck would be difficult to remove before he was ready to go, and she felt drained of emotion and too weary to insist. She shook her head. 'I don't know anything, Shane only mentioned him last night.'

'I presume he'll be on stage at the concert.'

'I presume so.'

'Are you going up to London for the show?'

'Yes.'

'How's Shane progressing with that opera of his?'

Rhiannon fidgeted with her hair. 'He's had some flashes of inspiration, but he's had no time yet for a concentrated effort. After the concert he'll be busy completing the album, and then there's the Far Eastern tour. I guess it will be a long time before he finally gets down to work.' And when he does, I shan't be around, she thought listlessly. He'll be finished with Submission, and me.

'Are you feeling all right?' Buck asked worriedly.

She lifted her chestnut head with the two bobbing bunches and gazed at him with wide, troubled eyes.

'I'm fine,' she lied. 'Just tired.'

'You won't consider an article on being married to the mean, moody and magnificent monster, then?'

She forced a thin smile. 'No. I'd rather keep our private life private.'

'Don't tell a soul I said this,' Buck bent his blond head to hers in a gesture of confidence, 'but I don't blame you. I come across all types in the entertainment world, and I've got them neatly classified. Some are publicity freaks. They get a kick from revealing everything—their joys, their sorrows, the skeletons in the cupboard. They use reporters like psychiatrists, and parade their innermost feelings for all the world to read. But others, like Shane, have a natural reticence. It doesn't come easy for them to be acclaimed. At heart they know it's all a big con trick. The sooner Shane drags himself out of the public gaze the better—he hasn't the inflated ego that superstars need.' He rose from the table. 'Thanks for the coffee and the chat. I won't use any of it.'

Rhiannon smiled gratefully.

'Don't think too badly of me.' Buck swung his legs into the low sports car. 'I have to stick my neck out at times, though I hate myself for doing it. I can't afford to be subtle, after all I have to make a living too!'

Rhiannon waved goodbye. After he had gone she pottered around the house. Shane rang in the evening, and in the background she could hear the babble of conversation and laughter.

'I'm having dinner at the hotel with Tony and Eddie,' he explained. 'David's shot off somewhere with Cheryl, so we poor neglected fellows thought we'd drown our sorrows together. How are you?'

'Tired. I'm going to bed early. How's Peter Willans shaping up?'

'He's great.' There was a note of relief in Shane's voice, 'You'll see him on stage. He's tall and blond, with a moustache, like a young Robert Redford. The girls'll flip over him, and he plays a mean piano.'

'He sounds perfect. Perhaps I'll seduce him when I've finished with you,' Rhiannon said flippantly. There was silence. Please say something, she implored silently. Please commit yourself, one way or the other, don't leave me in limbo. But Shane made no comment.

'See you at the concert,' she gulped eventually, despising herself. Why didn't I have the courage to spell out the future loud and clear? she wondered crossly, when their conversation had ended and she had replaced the receiver. Why didn't I make it plain I would be interested in other men once the agreement comes to an end? She knew the answer—it would not be true.

It was early next morning when the telephone rang, and as she lifted the receiver she was surprised to hear Buck's voice.

'You're not going to like this, Rhiannon,' he said, 'but I'm doing you a favour by warning you first. I presume you haven't seen this morning's paper?'

'No.'

'Well, it won't be long before your phone is buzzing with reporters asking for a comment on the photograph in it. If I were you I'd leave the receiver off the hook. I doubt anyone will bother to drive down to Sussex to interview you.'

'What photograph?'

'Your monster and Maxine.' The words fell about her like stones.

'Oh!'

'I'm ringing off now,' Buck said gently.

'Oh,' she repeated stupidly, as slow, certain pain infiltrated her being. Automatically she thanked Buck, though she didn't know what for, then hurriedly she broke the connection and laid the receiver down on the highly polished oak chest. She felt numb. She went upstairs to dress, pulling out the first thing that fell beneath her hands. It was a long-sleeved shift in cream jersey. She left her hair loose, and carefully made up her eyes. The face she presented to the world was composed, but inside she felt sick. What a splendid actor Shane was; he was wasting his time as a musician. He had convinced her he loved her, while all the time he'd been stringing her along, using her. Now it was obvious their marriage vows meant nothing to him.

'Please leave the phone off the hook, Mrs Jackson,' she called as she ran downstairs. 'I'm going into the village to buy a newspaper—I suppose I should arrange to have one delivered.' But she didn't. After she'd seen the photograph and read the caption she decided she never wanted to read another newspaper again. She brought the paper home and ran upstairs with it to the bedroom, where she spread it out on the white lace coverlet, to gaze at the incriminating evidence. Shane was sat at a dinner table, a cigar casually between his long fingers, with Maxine draped seductively over his shoulder. She was smiling into the camera, the curves of her décolletage prominently displayed, and an arm possessively around Shane's shoulders. His face was carefully noncommittal.

'Magnificent Shane Santiago dining with old flame, top model Maxine Daniels,' the caption shouted in heavy black letters. Beneath was a short paragraph detailing the forthcoming London concert and projected tour of the Far East. 'Mr Santiago declined to comment on his relationship with Miss Daniels. It is understood his bride of three months, Rhiannon, is supervising their home in Sussex.'

Rhiannon let out a muffled yell of rage, and ripped viciously at the paper until it lay in shreds about her feet.

'How could he?' she muttered to herself, as a wave of sheer fury shook her body. *He had no right to treat her like this*. She was filled with the need to destroy something, preferably Shane, but he wasn't there. Presumably he was still enjoying his grand reunion with Maxine. Well, if she couldn't destroy Shane, she'd destroy his house. She'd drag the pictures from the walls, smash the vases, mutilate the furniture, break the porcelain, hammer at the notes on his precious piano and burn all his music. She fell, face down, on to the bed, deaf, dumb and blind with misery. *She hated him.* She would destroy his beautiful home, which she had created. But as the tears retreated and her trembling body calmed, she knew she was fooling herself. She could never destroy anything, she wasn't selfish enough. She cared too much.

There was only one route left open to her, she decided, as the excess of emotion drained away. She must leave him. She wasn't prepared to continue their relationship any longer. From the very beginning it had been based on lies and coercion, and if he wanted to go to Maxine—well, let him! There was no way she could continue to pretend everything was satisfactory with their marriage when Shane's heart was, so obviously, in another place.

She would pack her belongings, load them into the car, and drive away. She could arrange to leave the saloon somewhere for him to collect later. Surely she would be happier away from Shane, his lies and infidelities? But where could she go? If she suddenly arrived at her parents' home and announced that her marriage was in shreds the shock might trigger off heart trouble for her father, and she couldn't risk that. Equally she couldn't stay with Anne in London, Shane would surely find her there. She wiped away her tears with a tissue, and noisily blew her nose. She would go to Scotland and stay in some anonymous hotel, she decided, sitting up straight, her mind crystal clear. She would wait until Mrs Jackson finished for the day, then pack the car, and at first light in the morning she'd be off. It was a long drive north, but if she started early she could do it in one day. Once her plan of action was decided she was filled with a cool detachment. The ambivalent emotions which Shane inspired had been resolved, and it was a relief to have finally reached a decision.

She repaired her tear-stained face and drove into town. There she visited the bank and drew out enough to last her for a week or two. After that she would find a job and be independent of Shane! Then she bought fresh fruit, bread and cheese to take on the journey; she didn't want to waste time stopping at cafés. When she returned home Mrs Jackson had left for the day, and she had the house to herself. She packed her clothes into two suit-cases and carried them down to the car, then she prepared a flask of coffee and composed a carefully worded note for Mrs Jackson, explaining that she was going away, but that Shane would return in a day or two. She deliberately made it vague, not saying where she was going, or when she was coming back. She walked carefully round the house, locking all the windows. An overnight bag was open in the bedroom to receive her toothbrush and other last-minute items. It was too painful to write a note of farewell to Shane, so she postponed the trauma by adding a P.S. to Mrs Jackson's note—'Will write to Shane in a day or two.' Finally she drove down to the local garage and filled the tank with petrol.

It was early evening when she pulled back into the drive. She was surprised to see a strange car parked before the front door, but there was no one around. She wondered if, despite Buck's words, some reporter had driven down from London to try and interview her about the newspaper photograph. Possibly someone was at the rear of the house poking around. Quickly Rhiannon opened the front door and slipped into the hall, locking the door behind her. She was in no mood for another inquisition. She went into the kitchen, meaning to peer out unobserved for an intruder in the back garden, when she stopped dead in her tracks. Shane sat at the table, scanning the note she had written. He was breathing through his teeth in a soft, dangerous whistle. He stood up when he saw her, and the violence of the emotions which crossed his face made her draw back helplessly.

'Why has the phone been off the hook all day?' he demanded, towering above her dark and menacing. 'I've been worried sick about you! I tried to ring all morning, and in the end I abandoned rehearsals and drove down here in a hire car to discover what was the matter. When I arrived the house was deserted, and then I discovered this note,' he shook it angrily in her face. 'What do you mean—"Will write to Shane in a day or two"?' His lips were compressed into a tight, furious line. He crumpled the note in his fist and tossed it savagely aside.

'I'm leaving you,' Rhiannon told him, his anger fuelling her determination. 'You can rant and rave all you like, but I'm not staying around to be made a fool of. You couldn't wait until our marriage was finished before you returned to Maxine's arms, could you?'

'What the hell are you talking about?'

Rhiannon exploded, *'The photograph!'* she yelled, her face hot with fury, 'The photograph in the newspaper. I saw it!'

'What photograph?'

'Don't play dumb,' she snapped, her hair flying as she tossed her head. 'The one of you and Maxine together in a restaurant, with her half naked on top of you. You're a plausible character,' she sneered. 'You certainly had me fooled—I imagined you cared for me.'

'I do. And I haven't seen any photograph.' His voice was cool. 'Where is it?'

'I tore it up,' she cried. 'How do you think I felt when I opened the newspaper and there you were—my husband, in an embrace with another woman, for all the world to see!'

'There's obviously been some misunderstanding,' Shane said slowly, rubbing his temple with one finger, 'but I think I know what must have happened. When we were having dinner yesterday evening, just after I phoned you, Maxine walked in. I had no idea she was coming, she just appeared.'

'Like a genie out of a bottle,' Rhiannon sneered. 'And

then I suppose you casually invited her to join you?'

'No!' he said loudly, as his temper began to assert itself again. 'It's not at all what you imagine. She'd brought some photographer along with her, and he took a few shots while she lounged around. Eddie encouraged it, even though he detests her. He said it was good publicity for the concert.'

'So you sat there complacently, while Maxine seduced you!'

'We were in a hotel dining room! Once she'd had her photograph taken she went away again. She was photographed with Tony as well, not just me, and,' Shane added, 'I most certainly did not go to bed with her, if that's what you're thinking.'

'What about the write-up?' Rhiannon demanded. 'Where did that come from?'

'I've no idea,' he said, with pronounced patience, as though dealing with a dimwitted child. 'What did it say?'

'That while you and Maxine were living it up in London, I was keeping house down in Sussex.' The words tumbled out one after the other in her distress. 'I think that's all you married me for, to straighten out the house for you!'

'Don't forget the legalised sex,' Shane drawled, his eyes glittering dangerously with scarcely suppressed rage, 'which you happen to enjoy as much as I do.'

Rhiannon bit her lip.

'Let's get this into perspective,' Shane said grimly. 'You should know better than to believe everything you read in the papers. For heaven's sake, you've been connected with the entertainment business long enough, you know how everything is distorted.'

'That's a convenient get-out,' Rhiannon flashed. 'Blame it on the press!'

He ignored her remark. 'It's obvious Maxine has been causing trouble, but you know what she's like,' he continued. 'She's hooked on publicity. She becomes depressed if her name or photograph isn't in the gossip columns at least once a week. In all probability she telephoned the newspaper and provided the print and report singlehanded.'

'I don't believe you!'

Shane moved his shoulder a fraction of an inch in an elegant shrug. 'Use your common sense, my darling. Telephone Eddie, or Tony, they'll verify what I've told you.'

'They'd say whatever you told them to say!'

'You're determined not to believe me.' Shane's blue eyes hardened into steel. 'Do you want me to swear on the Bible? I will.'

Rhiannon cast him a vicious look, 'I don't care what you do, I'm going. I was planning to leave in the morning, but I'll go now.' She swung aside to go out of the door, but he grabbed her arm, his fingers biting into her flesh.

'No, you won't,' he said curtly. 'You're too upset. In your present mood you'd wrap the car around a tree at the first bend you came to.'

Rhiannon prised at his fingers in an attempt to free herself, but his grip was like iron.

'And if you leave me, and break our agreement, then I shall break the agreement too, and leave Submission immediately,' he threatened. 'That means the concert will be cancelled, because Peter isn't ready to replace me yet. Thousands of tickets will have to be refunded, and the group will have a bad press for reneging on a date. The fans won't like it either.' Shane was frostily in control of himself, spitting out the words like slivers of ice which penetrated her soul.

'*I hate you!*' Rhiannon twisted and turned in his arms in vain, struggling to break his grip.

'And another thing,' Shane continued smoothly, holding her tight with apparent ease, 'if you break up our marriage before the allotted time I shall give Buck Andrews the full inside story.'

Rhiannon gasped, 'You couldn't do that, Shane!'

'I could, and I would.'

'You're ruthless,' she moaned. 'I don't know why you married me in the first place.'

'You said it yourself,' his voice was rich with malice, 'for a housekeeper and legalised sex.'

Rhiannon lashed out at him in fury with her free hand, the palm striking his face viciously.

'I suppose I deserved that,' Shane muttered darkly, rubbing his cheek. 'But why did *you* marry *me*?'

Rhiannon watched in horror struck fascination as a red weal appeared on the smooth plane of his face. 'You forced me.'

He shook his head. 'I put pressure on you, but I know damn well you could have come up with an alternative proposition if you'd really wanted to—you're an intelligent girl. But you never made any other feasible suggestions,' he said thoughtfully. 'You agreed almost immediately.'

'I was trapped,' she declared. 'First of all Eddie said the group would collapse and there would be severe financial hardship if I didn't marry you and make you stay on with Submission, and then David came along.'

'And what did he say?'

'He told me he couldn't pay off the mortgage on our parents' home if you left, and also that he needed money to get married, because Cheryl was pregnant.'

'Cheryl isn't pregnant,' Shane snapped. 'Anyone can see that.'

'He said she was, and I believed him,' Rhiannon finished lamely.

'You never checked?' His words were an accusation.

'It all happened so quickly—I couldn't think straight. Everyone was pushing me to marry you in order to keep the group flourishing.'

'So you sold yourself to ensure the cash flow was healthy!' He gave a bark of mirthless laughter. 'Good God, I'm supposed to be the villain of the piece, but you calculatedly married me for money!'

'*No!*'

'You married me so that Eddie could store up a nest

egg for his old age, and David could finance houses for your parents and himself—how very philanthropic!' His tone was insulting, cold and mean. Rhiannon chewed at her lip. The facts he had related were true, but his version was distorted—or was it? She couldn't deny that she had been giving way to the financial needs of Eddie, David and all the others when she had decided to marry him.

'But you didn't love me!' she burst out in defiance.

Shane raised a cynical black brow. 'I wanted you. I couldn't help myself, I had to have you.'

'That's not the same as love,' she cried.

'It's a far better reason than totting up the pound notes,' he taunted. 'Wait until Buck Andrews hears about this. You won't be his golden girl any longer, he'll slot you away with all the other money-grabbers.'

'I'm not a money-grabber!'

'Not for yourself, maybe, but for others,' Shane said coldly. 'It's the same thing.'

'You've twisted everything around—it wasn't like that at all,' her voice was desperate.

'Oh no?' He lifted his lip into a sneer. 'And once you've made sure everyone has a healthy bank balance you'll move on to other charitable works, I presume?'

Rhiannon's head fell forward, hot tears stinging her eyes.

'And you'll stay here tonight, with me.' His words were a command. She knew what he meant; she would stay with him—in his bed.

'*No!*'

'Yes, you will,' he threatened softly, 'otherwise I telephone your reporter friend Buck Andrews.' He cupped her breast with his hand and squeezed it firmly. 'I've been away from you long enough. I certainly don't intend to drive all the way back to London this evening. I want more legalised sex.'

She struggled afresh in his arms. 'I despise you!'

'Perhaps it's a two-way feeling,' he said nastily, flinging open the kitchen door, 'but as you've already enriched everyone's coffers by making love to me on so many other rapturous occasions, one more time isn't going to hurt. Or at least, it won't if you co-operate.'

'There's no way I shall co-operate with you!' Rhiannon ground out, still struggling in his arms.

'Then I shall have to take you by force.'

'Please, Shane,' she begged, 'please leave me alone.'

'You'll like making love to me,' he snapped sarcastically. 'You always do.'

He flung her up the stairs ahead of him so roughly that she stumbled. When they reached the threshold of the bedroom she hesitated, but Shane pushed her forward and slammed shut the door.

'Take off your clothes,' he growled with leisurely menace, reaching down almost indolently to unfasten the buckle of his belt, 'or do you prefer me to undress you?'

Stiffly Rhiannon's fingers undid her hooks and fastenings as she dropped her clothes to the floor. All the time his eyes burned into her, daring her to resist. When they were both naked he ran his hands over her body, deliberately arousing her.

'You see,' a triumphant laugh vibrated in his throat, 'you *do* want me.' He watched as the dark, puckered skin of her nipples hardened at the rub of his thumbs. She closed her eyes. His hands tormented her breasts until they were swollen with desire.

'I hate you!' She turned her head away from his demanding mouth.

'Open your eyes,' he instructed. 'That's better. Did you know that when you're aroused they have gold flecks in them?'

'I hate you!'

'No, you don't,' he shook his black curly head slowly. 'Your body wouldn't blossom for me like this if you did.' Suddenly his voice was tender. 'Lie down, my darling.'

She lay down on the silken coverlet, her dark hair spread around her shoulders, her brown eyes huge and imploring. Shane sank down beside her, and she pushed her head into the pillow away from him.

'You want me,' he repeated, as her traitorous body rose and fell in tumult at the irresistible caress of his fingers.

'I hate you,' she muttered savagely, but her body cried out for him.

'And you want me.'

With a sob of despair Rhiannon turned to him and thrust an arm around his neck, dragging his hard body down upon hers. There were tears running down her cheeks. 'You bastard,' she groaned, as he possessed her.

Some time in the night, he left her, and when she awoke the following morning she was alone.

Her suitcases lay untouched in the boot of the car, and the coffee-filled flask waited on the kitchen worktop, but still Rhiannon hesitated, uncertain of the plan of action she should adopt. It was mid-morning and she was on her knees, weeding the flower bed, tugging at the illicit greenery as her mind churned over repeatedly. Yesterday everything had seemed so clear, but now the situation was different. Or was it?

'Look at that blackbird!'

Her thoughts were interrupted by Alan Jackson's exclamation. 'Isn't it a beauty, so black and glossy, and what a size! You could roast it for Christmas dinner!'

Rhiannon smiled, grateful for a break in her introspection. Alan was working a few yards away, briskly digging over a neglected patch of the vegetable garden, while the blackbird hovered near, watching out for worms with a beady eye. Suddenly it flew down on to the grass beside her, and strutted up and down, demanding her attention. Then it sprang and soared up into the wide blue sky. With a soil-spattered hand she pushed a loose strand of hair out of her eyes and leant back on her heels to watch the bird, enjoying its carefree existence. When it had gone she returned reluctantly to the weeding, and her thoughts. She was tempted to ignore Shane's threats, climb into the car and go. Surely he was bluffing? She knew last night she had caught him on the raw; he had been hurt and angry, his reaction caused by his distress at finding the house empty, and then reading her note. He was hot-tempered, and temperamental, but he certainly wasn't vindictive. In the past, despite his antipathy towards the entertainment world, he had always been reliable.

Rhiannon tried to convince herself that should the concert be cancelled it was hardly disastrous. Concerts had been cancelled before, by other groups, if not by Submission. But probably Eddie would take a chance and carry on with Peter Willans in Shane's role. The substitution might turn into a great success, and Shane's absence would be hardly noticed. And, if she was forced to, she could cope with the embarrassing press coverage which would accompany the exposure of their arranged marriage. For a moment her face grew hot and pink as she imagined Maxine's delighted response to the news. Yes, it would be unpleasant, but she would survive.

And yet, when she had almost decided to grab the keys and leap into the car, she hesitated, her thoughts annoyingly switching to the other side of the coin. She *had* given her undertaking to abide by the agreement, and most of the reasons for which she had originally signed were still valid. And suppose Eddie refused to go ahead with the concert? It was possible Shane had prophesied correctly when he said that a cancelled date would be disastrous for Submission.

She wondered whether Shane really would expose the true facts of their relationship, and squirmed at the thought. He hated publicity, surely he wouldn't deliberately seek the limelight? But she remembered his anger the previous evening, and couldn't decide what he would do. She knew she was capable of dealing with the press, but what about her parents' reaction? Her father was vulnerable to stress, and the thought of reporters clamouring at his door filled her with panic. She plucked half-heartedly at a curl of chickweed and her thoughts circled fruitlessly again. Life with Brad would have been much simpler, she thought ruefully, but she acknowledged that perhaps it would have been a trifle humdrum. He certainly would never have had the power to drive her to the heights, or plunge her to the emotional depths, as Shane did.

Perhaps, in all fairness, she had been too hasty in flinging the news of her intention to leave at Shane. He had seemed stunned at her decision. Perhaps he had been telling the truth about his encounter with Maxine. She recognised that the impact of the newspaper photograph had rashly prompted her to attack him, and he had attacked back impulsively, caught up in the emotional exchange.

'Telephone!' shouted Mrs Jackson from the kitchen window, and Rhiannon stood up and stretched her legs. She brushed at the dirty patches on the knees of her trousers, and wiped her hands on her bottom before going into the house. As she lifted the receiver her heart thumped so noisily she thought it would drown out any conversation. Please let it be Shane, ringing to apologise. She crossed her fingers and wished, but it was Eddie.

'How are you?'

'Fine,' she replied, waiting for more. It was the morning of the concert, and she knew from past experience that Eddie would be chin-high in last-minute arrangements for crowd control, security, lighting, sound and another hundred and one worries. He certainly didn't have time to spare to telephone merely to enquire about the state of her health.

'What have you done to Shane?' he demanded, going straight for the jugular. 'He walked out of rehearsals in mid-flight yesterday, and this morning he's like a bear with a sore head. I've never known him in such a foul mood. No one can get a civil word out of him. What's the problem?'

'He's uptight about the concert.'

'*And?* There's more to it than that. I won't have him jeopardising Submission with this kind of behaviour, we've had too much aggro from him already this morning. He must calm down before the concert—you can almost see his tension coming out at you like laser beams. Something must be done. What time will you be arriving?'

'I'm not.'

'What!' Eddie nearly had an apoplexy. 'You *must*!'

'My presence wouldn't make any difference, in fact it might make things worse.'

'If this is some kind of lovers' tiff, I wish you'd picked another time,' Eddie said wearily. 'You'll just have to swallow your pride, Rhiannon, and make it up.'

'It's not a tiff, it's far more deep-rooted than that.'

'Hold on a minute. I'll call Shane, and he can have a word with you. Try and sort things out, please, for me, for Submission. I'm sure Shane would calm down if you were here.'

'Leave it, Eddie.' Rhiannon pulled at her hair agitatedly with earth-stained fingers. 'I'm sorry Shane is in a lousy temper, but, believe me, I can't help.'

'I'll ask him to telephone you.'

'*No*. Keep out of it. He won't let you down, he never has. He might moan and groan, but he always delivers the goods in the end. He'll glower at the audience and they'll melt in his hand.'

'Thank heavens Peter is a darn sight more amenable,' Eddie sighed. 'I'll tell Shane you're not coming. I just hope you're right about him not letting us down.'

'Keep quiet, say nothing, don't mention my name to him.'

'Okay,' he agreed reluctantly, but it was only ten minutes later, as she was drinking coffee with Mrs Jackson and Alan, when the telephone rang again. Before she lifted the receiver she knew it would be Shane. Eddie would have been unable to resist interfering and trying to smooth things over.

'I've been speaking to Eddie,' Shane said, with no preamble. 'He reckons you're not coming up for the concert this evening.'

'I'm not.' Nervously she licked her bottom lip with the tip of her tongue.

'I want you to come, I need you here.' For a moment there was a touch of intimacy in his tone, but then his arrogance clicked back into place and he was briskly formal, obviously unprepared to plead, or even ask nicely, she thought with a stab of pique.

'If you drive up straight away you'll be here just after two. I'll be expecting you. Come straight to the concert hall.'

'No.' Rhiannon's voice shook a little. 'What's the point? We'd only fight, and besides, my presence makes no difference to the fans, or the way you feel about being on stage.'

'It does,' he insisted harshly. 'It makes one hell of a difference. You want everything to turn out right, don't you?' His voice was brushed with malice, and Rhiannon sighed. They were right back where they had started, Shane issuing his demands while she had little alternative but to submit.

'I must go now,' he said tersely. 'They're yelling for me to get back on stage, we're in the middle of a new number.' He paused for a second, and then, very softly, said, 'Please come.'

CHAPTER SEVEN

IT was the note of raw desperation in the final two words that persuaded her. For a long moment she stood by the telephone, telling herself she was being weak and stupid, that she would do better to ignore Shane's plea and return to the garden. Then, with a sigh, she dismissed her doubts and ran quickly upstairs to shower. She shampooed her hair and blow-dried it, leaving the bouncy locks full and loose around her shoulders. After a moment's deliberation she decided to wear a black wool trouser suit, which she teamed with a white silk shirt, cut in a Victorian style, with a high ruffled neck. Dubiously she eyed the slender, spiky heels of her black suede boots—could she drive in them? She decided, with a hint of exasperation, that she could, and pulled them on, smoothing them tightly around her slender calves. She made up her eyes with dark violet shadow, and when she brushed mascara on to her long lashes, her eyes resembled mysterial dark pools in the paleness of her face. She slicked on lip-gloss and looked in the mirror. She needed to look good to boost her wavering morale, and after a quick, satisfied nod of approval, she went downstairs.

She poked her head round the kitchen door and spoke to Mrs Jackson. 'I'm going up for the concert now. Please would you lock up when you leave? We won't be home until late tonight.' The older woman had her hands deep in soapy water, and turned to look at Rhiannon over her shoulder.

'Give my love to Shane,' she instructed. 'I'm looking forward to seeing him again tomorrow. I'll bet he has those fans of his screaming tonight, he's such a handsome fellow.'

Rhiannon gave a soft snort. So Mrs Jackson had

fallen for his charms too!

Initially, as she drove through the country lanes she felt she had made the right decision by agreeing to attend the concert, but as the miles ticked over her mind began to prick with misgivings. By the time she reached the outer suburbs of London she was distinctly uneasy. Had the desperation in his voice merely been a figment of her imagination? She thought again of the newspaper photograph. His explanation had been totally void of guilt, and she knew it was feasible—many things were distorted by the press. But perhaps Maxine had been telling the truth when she said she and Shane had never really ended their association? And hanging ominously over everything, like a huge, dark cloud, was Shane's one comment on the future—*that he was looking forward to the end of their marriage contract.*

She parked the car outside the concert hall. It was a chill, blustery afternoon, and as she walked across the empty tarmac, the wind whipped at her hair, blowing it wildly across her face. She turned up the collar of her jacket for protection, and pushed her hands into her jacket pockets. Although the concert was not due to start until eight o'clock that evening, security guards were already in position. They had been on duty since early morning, keeping away the more persistent fans. Obviously they had been effective, for the entrance to the vast concert hall was deserted, though when Rhiannon approached the main door a guard stepped out from a booking kiosk where he had been keeping warm.

'I'm Shane Santiago's wife,' she told him, feeling a peculiar twist of pain and pleasure at the words.

'Go right in,' he held the door open wide. 'I was told to look out for you.'

Rhiannon walked past him into the gloom of the auditorium. The seats were on three levels, stretching in a wide semi-circle before the stage. She paused, allowing her eyes to adjust to the dim light, and watched briefly as a gang of cleaners brushed the carpet and cleared the ashtrays in preparation for the evening's army of fans. She walked slowly down the incline, between the rows of empty seats. One or two people she didn't recognise sat idly watching Submission, who were in the middle of a song which had reached number one in the charts the previous year. She hesitated, and slipped into an aisle seat. No one took any notice of her. There was no glamour to accompany the rehearsals, no air of excitement; even Cheryl and Kim, singing in harmony at the side of the stage, would not have merited a second glance in their baggy sweaters and slacks. The music sounded somewhat mundane, Rhiannon thought, as it rang around the empty theatre. No matter what Shane felt, the fans were necessary to provide the magic, the hidden ingredient that changed a collection of music into a throbbing evening of delight.

Her heart fluttered foolishly when she saw him, and she folded her arms and told herself not to be so emotional. She was a grown woman, not a lovelorn schoolgirl. Shane was bending over the keyboard, deep in concentration, his black tee-shirt emphasising the strength and width of his shoulders, and his tight denim jeans moulding the muscles of his long legs. He was big and strong and powerful. Rhiannon fingered the diamond solitaire at her throat. Eddie had been correct when he had said Shane's tension was visible. It was there for everyone to see in the taut set of his jaw, the way he suddenly thrust back the fall of thick, dark hair from his brow with an impatient gesture.

In contrast a blond young man, playing a keyboard on the opposite side of the stage, was completely relaxed, his foot tapping in time to the beat, a happy grin on his face. That must be Peter Willans, she decided. He *was* attractive. It was easy to see from his attitude that he was delighted to be a member of Submission, but his pleasure was more than that. He was, like David, an extrovert, and as the music stopped he winked at one of the women cleaners, and gave a wide smile before sauntering over to talk to Kim. Rhiannon looked back at Shane. He pushed his hands into the back pockets of his jeans and frowned, his stiff posture yelling out, 'For heaven's sake, let's get this over with, I've better things to do.'

Rhiannon sighed. She had been wrong to come, she decided with a terrifying contraction of her heart. It was blatantly obvious that Shane's tenseness at appearing on stage had returned, and that, coupled with his anger at her threat of leaving him, made the prospect of a confrontation worrying, to say the least. And what could she say? Her thoughts were still frantically spiralling, and she was beginning to lose patience with both herself and Shane.

'That's it, lads, back for the show around seven-thirty,' shouted the leader of the band, and with a sigh of relief the musicians put down their instruments and began to move away from their seats, some to stretch and yawn, others to grab their jackets and disappear. Rhiannon stood up and swallowed hard before making her way towards the stage. Shane's face brightened for an instant when he saw her, but then a careful mask of control dropped into place.

'Thank you for coming,' he said, kissing her briefly on the forehead. 'Come into my dressing room, I want to talk to you.' It was more an order than a request, and her Welsh temper sparked at his authoritative tone. She was tempted to refuse, but after a moment's hesitation gave a small sigh and followed him. The dressing room was minuscule and shabby. If Shane had stretched out his arms in both directions he would have touched the walls with his fingertips. A large built-in wardrobe took up a third of the space, leaving room only for a dressing table and mirror, and two bentwood chairs. Shane closed the door and pulled out a chair for Rhiannon. He leant against the cream emulsioned wall and looked down at her, his eyes a disturbing shade of pale blue.

'I'm sorry about last night,' his voice was low and apologetic. 'I was uptight about the concert, and I

panicked when I couldn't contact you. I began to imagine you'd met with some kind of accident. When I
found the house empty I felt dreadful, and then I read
your note and I just went berserk.' He reached forward
and ran his fingers down the side of her face. Rhiannon
stiffened and pushed them away.

He drew back. 'You're not prepared to forgive me?'

She shook her head. 'It's not that simple, Shane, is
it?'

He shrugged, almost diffidently. 'I don't want to hurt
you.'

Rhiannon raised her large brown eyes in despair.
'Well, you do,' she said unevenly. 'I refuse to go on like
this. We must talk and clear the air.'

'Not now,' he groaned, rubbing his forehead. 'I'm
already as taut as a violin string as it is. Let's leave it.
Tomorrow we'll sit down quietly at home and talk things
over with no interruptions. We'll plan the future.'

She noticed, irritably, that he had said *the* future, not
our future. It was the last straw. 'There is no future,' she
snapped, 'at least, not for us.'

Shane sucked in a breath of air through clenched
teeth. 'Is that what you want?' he asked quietly, with an
almost menacing air, 'a separate future?' He took a step
towards her, then suddenly, before Rhiannon could
reply, stopped and put his head on one side, listening
carefully. 'What was that?'

'What?'

'A noise. It came from the wardrobe, I think.'

With one swift movement he reached across and flung
wide the door to reveal Betsy huddled among the
clothes.

'What the hell are you doing here?' he demanded,
pulling the girl out into the room. Rhiannon watched
on in astonishment. Betsy giggled, a dark red flushing
across her face as she played sheepishly with the zip of
her nylon anorak.

'I'm sorry, but I wanted to have a peep into your
dressing room,' she confessed. 'I've never seen a dressing

room before. But then I heard voices, so I hid.'

'And listened in to our entire conversation!' Shane accused angrily.

'I didn't know you were going to talk. I didn't like to come out once you'd started. I'm sorry your marriage isn't going well.'

'*Shut up!*' Shane spat out the words with such fury that Betsy paled visibly. 'Our marriage is none of your concern, so just keep out of it. We don't need you around, we're perfectly capable of sorting things out for ourselves.' He opened wide the dressing room door. 'Now *get out*. I don't like girls who eavesdrop. Having you around is worse than inviting the C.I.A. to sit in on my life!'

'I didn't hear all your conversation, only the bits when you both raised your voices,' Betsy assured him. Shane turned his back, dismissing her with an angry movement of his broad shoulders.

The girl scuffed the toe of her wedge-heeled shoe on the floor.

'You're always getting rid of me,' she said defiantly. 'You should be nice to me.'

'I should be nice to you!' Shane spun round in rage and glowered at her. 'I probably would be if you didn't sneak into my bedroom and my dressing room, and listen in to private conversations between Rhiannon and me. You're always intruding. Why the hell do you imagine we hire security guards? It's so we can have some measure of privacy, which you most certainly do not respect.' He jerked his head. 'Now get out before I call the guard.'

'I'm going,' Betsy assured him with a disdainful glance, 'but I shan't bother to come to your show this evening.'

'Thank goodness,' Shane said heavily. He watched the girl's sullen progress down the corridor until the door closed behind her, then turned again to Rhiannon. 'This obviously isn't the place to talk,' he muttered, his eyes gritty with irritation. Then he sighed. 'Here's Eddie now, what does he want?'

The older man appeared at the door of the dressing room, and gave Rhiannon a grateful smile before turning to Shane. 'Can you spare a moment to try on your new costume? There was a hitch in delivery, but the seamstress is here now, and she says if the suit doesn't fit she can alter it on the spot, ready for tonight's performance.'

Shane looked puzzled. 'I didn't know we were having new costumes.'

'Sorry, it must have slipped my mind. I thought the image needed updating. The new outfits create more of an impact, add a touch of drama. The white suits were becoming passé.'

Shane gave a shrug of resignation. 'Let's have a look.'

The seamstress deposited a large cardboard box on the floor, and proceeded to unfold layers and layers of tissue paper, until finally she extracted a one-piece jump-suit in silver lamé. It had long sleeves, padded shoulders and a zip from neck to crotch. She stood on tiptoe and held it up high on its hanger for everyone to see.

Shane stared at it in amazement for a stunned moment, and then burst out laughing. 'Good God, Eddie, you don't expect me to wear *that*!' He put out a hand and rubbed the material between two fingers. 'It's elasticated!'

'Sexy,' ventured the seamstress.

'Very tight,' snapped Shane, rounding on Eddie. 'And that's the whole idea, isn't it, to sell sex? Well, count me out. I don't give a damn what David and Tony wear, but there's no way you're getting me into that thing.' He poked at it irritably. 'I'm not going on stage with my pelvis outlined for every teenage girl to fantasise over.'

'Try it on,' Eddie wheedled. 'It'll look better when you're in it. It's not that tight.'

'I'm not going to prance around, looking like something from outer space, and that's final!' Shane glared disgustedly at the silver suit.

As Eddie started up with a fervent mixture of pleas and threats Rhiannon left them. She had no desire to become involved in another argument. She walked across the stage to talk to David, who greeted her happily.

'Cheryl's looking radiant for a decidedly unpregnant lady,' she commented drily, after his greeting.

He laughed goodnaturedly, and put his arm around her, 'We all make mistakes. Come and meet our new man.' Peter Willans was quick-witted and humorous, and with an acid turn of mind Rhiannon decided that if, in due course, she was to be transferred to him, perhaps she could do worse. After chatting with the two men for several minutes she excused herself and returned to the dressing room, but it was empty.

'Where's Shane?' she asked Eddie, who was still talking to the seamstress.

'Gone.'

'Where?'

'Heaven knows, perhaps back to the hotel.' Eddie wearily wiped a handkerchief over his face.

'When will he be back?'

'I don't know. We had a row. He refused to wear the jump-suit, and I lost my temper and told him if he didn't then he could count himself out of Submission. He said that was just what he wanted, and off he went.'

Rhiannon rubbed her brow in annoyance.

'But we need him,' Eddie continued worriedly. 'Peter is good, but he isn't ready to take over yet. Besides, Shane's billed to appear and that's who the fans will demand. If you could persuade him to come back I'd be eternally grateful. I know I shouldn't have tried to force him to wear the suit, but we're both on edge at present with the strains of the show, and it all became rather heated.'

'I can imagine.' Her tone was clipped.

'There's always the chance he might return on his own. We've had arguments before, but he's never missed a performance. There's something else worrying him, it's not just the show. What's the matter between the two of you?'

Rhiannon examined the toe of her boot. 'We had a row,' she confessed. 'I saw that newspaper photograph of Maxine oozing all over him. I didn't like it, and I got mad.'

Eddie gave a bark of laughter, 'You didn't imagine that was for real, did you? Tony and I were there too, you know. The hussy just walked in and started leaning all over the guys. The next thing we knew a photographer was running around, letting off flashbulbs. But I went along with it because I reckoned it was good publicity. Shane was furious. He told Maxine where to get off in no uncertain manner—I doubt she'll dare to trouble him again.'

Rhiannon sucked at her bottom lip. So her accusations had been unjust, and she, in part, was responsible for Shane's behaviour.

'I'll try and find him,' she offered. It seemed the least she could do.

'That's a good girl! Tell him he can wear whatever he wants—his jeans if he must. Off you go now, and see if you can talk some sense into him.'

Shane was not at the hotel. His room was empty, and the desk clerk reported that Mr Santiago had not yet returned. Rhiannon sat herself down in the lobby on a red velvet chair, and wondered where to start her search. The concert was due to begin in four hours' time, and Shane could be anywhere. Possibly he had grabbed a taxi, or boarded a plane. He never did things by half, and in his present mood he was capable of anything. The hotel lobby was grand, with oak-panelled walls and a high, arched ceiling. At one end was a spectacular stained glass screen, reminiscent of a church. She suddenly remembered how Shane had said he sometimes visited a churchyard in the centre of London when he wanted to think. She sat up straight. It was a long shot, but possibly he might be there.

It took over an hour to locate the churchyard. She wandered around the streets in the vicinity of Shane's former apartment, but everyone she asked was either a visitor to London, or had no knowledge of the church. Finally, feeling cold and dispirited, she approached a road sweeper, and he was able to give explicit directions. Within minutes she found the tiny church. Tentatively she walked beneath the wooden archway and through the overgrown churchyard, where ancient, tottering gravestones seemed to be held upright only by the tangle of brambles that rampaged over them. The gravel path she walked along was in danger of disappearing completely into the undergrowth of long grass and bracken, but the tumbledown graveyard had charm. Rhiannon could understand why it appealed to Shane. It was a resilient oasis in the midst of the ever-changing life of the twentieth century. Its very existence was proof of permanence and security, and that was what Shane needed. With a sudden flash of insight, she recognised that his hostility towards his position as a pop star was caused by a basic lack of assurance about himself, his roots, his background. His arrogant control was a façade, beneath which was a man in search of himself. Rhiannon frowned. She had almost completed the short circuit around the tiny church, with its peeling, brown-painted doors, when she saw him. He was sat grimly on an old wooden bench, his elbows on his knees, his head in his hands. He looked up as she approached and gave a half smile. Then he twisted his wrist, and looked at the heavy watch. 'Don't worry. There's plenty of time before curtain up. I wouldn't let them down. I might huff and puff in great style, but that's about all I do. Apart from creating one God-awful mess and ruining our relationship,' he added bitterly.

Rhiannon sat down beside him and laid a hand on his bare wrist. He was without a jacket, and his skin felt icy to the touch, for there was a cool wind, and the weak, late afternoon sun held little warmth in its pale golden rays.

'You have goose pimples,' she said.

He shuddered. 'I'm frozen.' He rubbed his forearms up and down rapidly in an attempt to warm himself. 'I've been here for ages. I came straight from the theatre. I've worked everything out,' he turned to her and took hold of her hands. 'I've been handling the whole set-up very badly, but I know where I've gone wrong, and I intend to set things right.' He sighed. 'I don't know how you've put up with me.'

'It's not been all bad,' she protested. 'We've shared some wonderful moments, and it's fun furnishing the house.'

His face cleared. 'Yes, at least there's no problem there. I'm sorry I'm so moody at the moment, but I'm on edge with the show. You'd imagine because I've done so many that I'd be used to them by now, and could take them in my stride, but it gets worse. I can feel the tension building up inside me, and I feel positively sick at times. I try and keep calm, believe me,' he added, squeezing her hand so tightly it hurt. 'I have a great psychological barrier about going on stage and having thousands of pairs of eyes trained on me. It must be stage fright.' He shook his dark head in bewilderment. 'Tony and David don't feel like that. It's an ego trip for them, being on stage gives them a kick.' He lifted her hand to his mouth and kissed her fingertips. 'It might not seem like it, but being married to you has made one hell of a difference. I relax when I'm with you. I feel comfortable, whereas before I was continually uneasy. Now I forget about the pressures most of the time, but these last few days, when you weren't here . . .' His voice faded.

'We'll sort things out,' Rhiannon assured him tenderly.

'I hope so, my darling, I really hope so.'

He glanced at his watch and stood up abruptly, pulling Rhiannon to her feet. 'We'd better go back to the hotel, and I'll change. I'll wear my white suit.' He grinned ruefully. 'I reckon Eddie will have realised by now that I'm not happy with the Star-trek outfit.'

Rhiannon linked her arm through his as they walked towards the exit. 'He said you could wear whatever you wanted.'

'How about a bell tent?'

The concert was a resounding success. Rhiannon stood in the wings with Eddie and watched as Submission went faultlessly through their hit songs and latest numbers. At the end of each item there was loud applause, whistles and shouts, and then prolonged applause again when the first notes of the next song hit the air.

'What did I tell you?' she grinned, squeezing Eddie's arm. 'Shane was fine.'

'He did manage the occasional smile,' Eddie agreed, 'even though it was to you, offstage.' He rubbed his chin. 'I hate to admit it, but I think he was right about the silver gear. It does look weird, not classy enough for Submission.' He wrinkled his nose. 'But we'll have to have new outfits for the Far East.'

'Consult Shane this time,' Rhiannon warned. She peered through a gap in the curtains. 'I can't see Betsy, can you? She usually has a seat on the front row. She must be carrying out her threat not to come.'

'She'll be around somewhere—no show without Punch!'

'I wish Shane hadn't been quite so brusque with her this afternoon.'

'He had every right to be,' Eddie's reply was indignant. 'That girl breaks all the rules. We spend thousands of pounds on security, and then she turns up hiding in a wardrobe like a Peeping Tom! If I'd found her I'd have slung her out personally, and given her a good talking to. She'd not have come back in a hurry.'

'But she only wanted to see the dressing room.'

Eddie gave an impatient grunt. 'Yes, and Shane.'

'Perhaps.'

'No "perhaps" about it. She's up to her old tricks again. You'd think she would have found something better to do by now. Still, no doubt she'll come to her senses eventually. Her home life must be pretty drastic if she feels compelled to escape it by following Submission around. What kind of parents would allow their daughter to trail after a pop group?'

'Maybe they don't care,' Rhiannon said thoughtfully. 'I shouldn't think they do.'

A few minutes prior to the end of the last number, Rhiannon made her way out to a black limousine which was waiting in the car park. She settled herself in the back seat.

As soon as the final number ended, the stage lights would be doused and Submission would run from the concert hall, directly into waiting cars, to be driven away before the fans realised they would not be returning for a final encore. David and Tony would be taken home to their city apartments, while Shane and Rhiannon would be delivered to the hotel. There Shane would change, and then they would collect their car from the hotel basement and drive home to Sussex. The uniformed chauffeur touched his cap, and glanced through the mirror. 'He's here,' he said, and twisted round to open the rear door. Shane jumped in, flushed and panting. As he sank back beside Rhiannon, his chest heaving, the chauffeur turned the key, and the car shot forward. Rivulets of sweat coursed down Shane's face, running down his throat into the mat of dark hair on his chest. He peeled off his jacket, and the midnight blue shirt beneath was stained with dark patches of perspiration. He grinned. 'It was hot out there tonight under all the lights,' he said, fingering the black curls which were plastered wetly to his cheeks. 'Everything went off fine, didn't it? I thought Peter made a great debut, the new songs were well received, and I behaved myself. What a day!' He pulled out a white handkerchief and mopped his damp brow.

'You're impossible!' Rhiannon exclaimed. His moodiness had vanished, and now he was high on happiness.

'And you're sweaty and horrible, and . . .'

'*And* you love me?' Shane finished off for her, with a grin. '*And* you hate me, *and* you want me?' His look was challengingly provocative, and she felt as though his blue eyes, with their sensual message, were penetrating her soul. She remembered how he had ruthlessly aroused her the previous night, and was flooded with a sudden desire for this infuriating man who could force her to experience so many conflicting emotions at one and the same time.

The pavements outside the hotel were crowded.

'For heaven's sake!' Shane swore softly under his breath. 'They can't all be here because of me!'

'I think there's been an accident, sir,' offered the chauffeur as they drew up outside the hotel entrance. 'Look, there's an ambulance parked in that side street, and a couple of police cars.'

'I wonder what's happened?' said Rhiannon as they climbed from the car. There were one or two casual glances in their direction as they pushed their way forward through the crowds, but no one paid them much attention. All eyes were riveted on a balcony, outside a hotel bedroom, about five floors up. Rhiannon peered into the night sky. A solitary figure, a woman in a skirt and sweater, was sitting precariously on the edge of the stone balcony, swinging her legs.

'Why doesn't the silly bitch jump?' someone in the crowd muttered nastily. 'Just enjoying the attention, that's all she's doing. She's been perched up on that ledge for ages.'

Rhiannon felt Shane's hand on her shoulder, guiding her gently forward. Together they made their way through the crowd of upturned faces into the lobby.

'There he is!' shouted the desk clerk as they entered, and Shane hesitated as a police inspector came forward.

'Are you Shane Santiago of Submission?'

Shane nodded, his face serious.

'Perhaps you could help us, sir. It's about that young lady out on the ledge.'

'Has that something to do with me?'

'I'm afraid so, sir. It's a girl called Betsy Clark, and she's threatening to jump off because you don't love her. She's not a girl-friend of yours, is she?'

'Heavens, no! She's a fan, a very persistent fan. In the past she's sent me letters and gifts, protestations of undying love,' Shane raised a worried brow. 'I've only met her a few times, very briefly. My wife is fully aware of the situation.'

Rhiannon stepped forward. 'It's the usual thing,' she explained. 'Betsy has a crush on Shane, though she hardly knows him. She spends most of her time following Submission around, but she's a young girl, she'll grow out of it.'

'If she lives that long,' commented the inspector drily.

Rhiannon shivered at his words.

'How can I help? What can I do?' Shane asked. 'Do you think she'd respond if I reasoned with her?'

'I don't know, sir. You can never tell in situations like this. It's more than likely she's just drawing attention to herself and doesn't intend to jump, but on the other hand she does sound very bitter about you. She's been almost hysterical at times, and that ledge is narrow. It only needs her to become distraught, and without meaning to, she could tumble off. We've been sitting it out for the last hour, hoping she'll become bored and see sense. How she got into your bedroom in the first place beats me.'

'Could I speak to her, Inspector?' Rhiannon suggested. 'She knows me slightly. I could tell her Shane was here.'

The policeman nodded, 'I think that would be a better approach than suddenly springing Mr Santiago on her.'

Swiftly they boarded the lift, and when they entered the bedroom the inspector introduced them briefly to three uniformed constables, a young policewoman, and the hotel doctor. There was a tense atmosphere as everyone waited. The policewoman resumed her perch on the window sill and made some placatory comments to an invisible Betsy.

'Keep your voices subdued,' the inspector instructed. 'The girl can't see you from here, but we can't take any chances. We don't want her to become confused or startled, so play it low key. No sudden movements, no sharp words, no ultimatums.'

'With respect, sir, I think we should rush her,' one of the constables suggested. 'I could be through the window and on to the balcony in a flash. She'd have no time to react, I'd take her by surprise.'

'You can't do that!' protested the hotel doctor, an elderly woman in a starched white cotton coat.

'I agree,' said the inspector firmly, 'it's too risky. The window is small, and you'd have little room to manoeuvre. She already has her legs over the edge of the balcony, she'd only need to lean forward and she could topple off. Mrs Santiago here has kindly offered to try and get her to talk to Mr Santiago. I think he's the one who could persuade her to come in.'

The policewoman stood aside, and Rhiannon took her place on the windowsill and leaned out, her heart thudding erratically. The balcony was purely ornamental, its stonework weatherbeaten, covered with pigeon droppings and years of London grime. Betsy was huddled on the far corner, diagonally across from the window. Her back was to the building, and she was shivering in the cold night air.

'Betsy!' Rhiannon called softly. 'It's me, Rhiannon.'

'Go away.' The girl's voice was low. She didn't bother to turn round.

'Don't feel bad about Shane,' Rhiannon continued, striving to keep her voice even, though her throat was painfully dry. 'He was in a bad temper, so perhaps he overreacted to discovering you in the wardrobe. He's always under tremendous strain before a concert—you know how the press says he's mean, moody and magnificent?' She gave a forced laugh. 'Today was one of his moody times, but he's over it now. The concert was a great success, I was sorry you missed it.'

Betsy turned a fraction to look over her shoulder. 'Did Shane notice I wasn't there?'

'Oh yes.' Rhiannon crossed her fingers at the lie. She was privately certain that Shane had never noticed Betsy's absence, he was too wound up on stage to casually inspect individual members of the audience.

'Shane doesn't like me much.' Betsy's voice quavered. 'Nobody likes me very much at all.'

'Nonsense,' Rhiannon said briskly. 'He's here now, and he wants to talk to you.'

The girl moved fretfully on the balustrade, making Rhiannon's heart leap to her throat. 'Nobody likes me,' she muttered. 'My mum and dad don't care about me, and neither does Shane. He just wants me out of his life.'

'No, he doesn't. He's temperamental, that's all. He gets mad rapidly, but cools down rapidly too. You should have heard him arguing about a silver jump-suit Eddie wanted him to wear for the concert! They had a furious row, but it's all forgotten now, and they're friends again.'

'Did he wear the silver suit this evening?' Betsy twisted round to face her.

'No, he wore the usual, but David and Tony were in the new gear.'

'I bet Shane looked better. He's so dashing in white. I have a huge poster on my bedroom wall of him in his suit with the dark blue shirt. I look at it every night before I go to sleep. It makes me have such lovely dreams about him.'

'He's wearing that outfit now, would you like to see him?'

'Yes, please!'

'I'll get him.'

Rhiannon stepped back into the room, and everyone looked at her expectantly. 'She seems calm enough. She'd like to speak with Shane.'

He breathed deeply and cracked his knuckles, his face pale and drawn. 'Fine,' he said, with at attempt at a smile. He walked over to the window, but instead of sitting on the sill, he bent his head and climbed through, out on to the balcony. Everyone in the room held their breath.

'Do you think she's genuine?' the inspector asked Rhiannon. 'I have a suspicion she's just using her contact with your husband to turn herself into something of a celebrity.' He shook his head. 'Perhaps I'm doing her an injustice. Certainly her mood is capricious. I just hope your husband can handle her.'

The room fell silent again. Rhiannon gripped her elbows, holding her arms against her body as she stood perfectly still, her ears alert for any sound. She could hear the murmur of Shane's voice, calm and persuasive, then Betsy's inaudible reply. The minutes ticked by like years. At one point Betsy's voice grew shriller, and everyone held their breath until Shane spoke again, low and firm, and gradually the girl's voice became more controlled. Then there were movements on the balcony and Betsy's pale face suddenly appeared at the window. With some help from the policewoman she clambered through, Shane close behind her. There was a faint ripple of applause from the spectators down below in the street. The woman doctor led Betsy to an armchair. For an instant she gazed around at all the policemen with terrified eyes as the enormity of what she had done suddenly frightened her, then she began to sob.

'There, there,' said the doctor gently. 'You need to rest for a while. You come with me to my office and you can lie down. I'll make you a cup of tea and give you something to quieten you.' She picked up her black leather bag and led Betsy away, a protective arm around her shoulders.

'Thank you, sir.' The inspector came forward to shake Shane's hand. 'All's well that ends well. Some of these girls will do anything to make contact with pop stars!'

'It was my fault she was out there in the first place.' Shane's voice was rough. 'She sneaked into my dressing room this afternoon, and I lost my temper and told her to get out. I had no idea she'd take it so hard.'

'Don't feel guilty, sir. We often deal with girls like Betsy, plain girls with empty lives. They sometimes use the threat of suicide as a way of adding a touch of drama to their dull existence. They latch on to a pop star, or an actor, build up a dream world in their heads and lose touch with reality. If they can forge a link with that celebrity they feel they've achieved something. Don't blame yourself, sir. If it hadn't been you, it would have been someone else. You were just an excuse. She was using you.'

'I wish I could believe that.'

'Do you know where the girl lives, sir?' the inspector asked. 'We'll have to arrange for her family to collect her.'

'She isn't close to her parents. She says they're totally uninterested in her. She doesn't want them to be informed.' Shane glanced ruefully across at Rhiannon. 'Betsy is coming home with my wife and me.' Rhiannon opened her eyes wide in surprise. 'She said nobody cared for her, so I told her she could come and stay with us for as long as she likes.'

CHAPTER EIGHT

'THANK you for your statements.' The young policeman closed his notebook with a snap. 'I'll go downstairs now and have a word with the young lady, and that should just about clear everything.'

'If you need more information from us, you have our address and telephone number,' Shane offered.

'Thank you, sir.'

When the policeman had gone Shane started unbuttoning his sweat-soaked shirt. 'I'll change, then we'd better check with the doctor that Betsy's fit to travel.' He glanced at his watch and pulled a face. 'Hell, it's almost one o'clock—I'm exhausted!'

Rhiannon sat wearily on the edge of the bed, and watched as he put on navy slacks and sweater. Then he started to collect his belongings and pack them into a grey leather suitcase. She twisted a curl of hair around her finger. 'Why on earth did you have to invite Betsy to come and stay with us?' she asked at last, with a touch of sharpness. 'You know you'll hate it.'

Shane lifted some shirts from a drawer and laid them on the bed. 'I had to offer something constructive,' he explained. 'She was very distressed. I talked and talked in an effort to calm her. To be honest, I can't remember half I said. Her plight really came home to me. Submission is her only interest, it's all she cares about.' He went into the bathroom for his shaving tackle, 'She has no friends, and her family life sounds lousy. Apparently her own mother died when she was a baby, and her stepmother ignores her. She has twin stepbrothers who are her parents' favourites, and they always come first. When she was younger she had to look after them, her parents used her as an unpaid housemaid. Now the boys are older and she rattles around the house like a spare part. She's no use to the family any more, and they make her feel she's in the way. I imagine that's why Submission plays such an important role in her life. We're a substitute. She directs all her frustrated love and affection towards the group.'

'Towards you,' Rhiannon said pithily. 'Here, let me help.'

Shane stood aside as she folded the shirts and laid them in the case. She picked up the discarded white suit and packed that, too. When she had finished Shane snapped down the locks and lifted the case from the bed.

'Cheer up,' he said with a wry smile at her melancholy expression. 'Betsy won't stay for long. You're tired, my love, things will look better in the morning.'

Rhiannon raised her eyes in despair. 'She might decide to stay for ever, a perpetual lodger!'

Shane laughed and put his arms around her, trying to cheer her up.

'Pessimist! Just wait. Once the first flush of enthusiasm at staying in the house of a real pop star has faded, she'll be off like greased lightning. Look on the bright side, you can always rope her in to help you with the garden. We'll buy another spade,' he joked. 'Perhaps I'll get myself a whip and oversee the pair of you!'

Rhiannon refused to be cajoled. 'Alan Jackson has done all the heavy work, and the garden's in good shape. We don't need any more workers. What'll we do with Betsy all day?'

'We won't *do* anything. We'll just include her in our normal everyday life. Don't worry. I shall be working at home for the next couple of weeks. I have to do the final arrangements for the remainder of the album tracks. After that she can come up to London with us, and see how we record at the studios.'

'Okay,' she admitted grudgingly, 'I suppose I'm being uncharitable.'

'Makes a change.' Shane's comment was ambiguous, and she flashed him a searching glance, but his face was expressionless. He slung his leather jacket casually over one shoulder and picked up the suitcase. 'All clear,' he announced, with a last quick look around the room. 'Let's go and collect our guest.'

Betsy was pale and subdued, but the doctor said she was fit enough to travel down to Sussex with them. She lay down on the back seat of the car, and snuggled down beneath a cosy woollen travelling rug. Within minutes of them leaving the basement car park she was fast asleep. Rhiannon leant over from the front seat and tucked the rug more securely around the sleeping girl's shoulders. The doctor had told them to keep her calm and quiet for a few days, to give her the opportunity to recover from any delayed shock. Rhiannon settled in her seat and looked ahead, through the windscreen, at the empty roads, which were dark and unreal, like a film set. They sped along through the city, and out into the suburbs. There was an occasional light in an upstairs window, but otherwise no sign of life.

'I hope you haven't set a precedent.' She twisted her lip, conscious of being unfair, but unable to stop herself. 'Perhaps hundreds of your fans will decide to dangle from balconies and then move in with us.' Her words were light, but Shane recognised the exasperation behind them. She felt sorry for Betsy, but she didn't want her sharing her home, she wanted to be alone with him. He glanced at her and pursed his lips, but said nothing. As they reached the wide, deserted lanes of the dual carriageway he accelerated, and the big car purred, its power easily eating up the miles.

'And what about clothes?' she chaffed. 'What will Betsy wear? I presume she didn't have her suitcase ready packed when you decided to offer her accommodation.'

'Don't be sarcastic.' Shane removed his hand from the steering wheel and squeezed her fingers briefly, but she failed to respond. 'She can borrow something of yours.'

'They'd never fit,' she retorted with peppery anger. 'She's much fatter than I am.' She cast a backward glance at Betsy's plump figure, deep in sleep.

'And not in such good shape, either,' Shane commented. 'Don't worry, we can buy her some new clothes.'

Rhiannon gave a loud, dissatisfied sigh. 'It'll be awful,' she complained tiredly. 'You were mighty generous, giving her free accommodation for the rest of her life!'

'Don't be childish. She'll soon become tired of life in the country and move on. In any case, I hadn't any alternative. I had to say something to persuade her to come off that balcony.'

'I'm surprised you didn't offer her a place in your bed, too,' she said nastily, her exhaustion souring her temper. 'I'm sure we could make room for her. You gave her board and lodging, why not a full package deal?'

Shane set his mouth in a tight line. 'Don't try my patience too far,' he warned. 'We're both worn out, and I don't want to argue, but if you don't shut up I shall stop this car, and spank that beautiful bottom of yours. I realise you don't welcome an intruder, and, believe me, neither do I, but we'll have to make the best of it. I feel guilty. It was my fault, in part, that Betsy was out on the ledge in the first place. It's the least I can do to try and help her resume a stable life again. She's not such a bad kid.'

Rhiannon clenched her teeth. She knew she was being unreasonable, but she had been so happy at the prospect of talking things over with Shane and trying to resolve their relationship. Now the girl's presence would spoil everything. And she had a sneaking suspicion Betsy had planned the whole charade as a means of getting close to Shane.

'You said yourself she was like the C.I.A.,' she reminded him tartly.

Shane gave an impatient grunt. 'Cut it out,' he ordered. 'She's coming to stay, that's all there is to it.'

They reached the house in record time. While Betsy slumped half asleep on the sofa, still drowsy from the sleeping pill the doctor had given her, Shane made hot milky drinks. Rhiannon went upstairs and prepared the spare bed. In her more fanciful moments she had imagined the room as a nursery, fresh and pretty in pastel shades with a lace-trimmed crib containing a tiny, dark-haired baby, but now it was to receive an eighteen-year-old girl, whom she hardly knew and whose presence she resented. She found a new toothbrush and a spare nightgown, and when they had finished their drinks she showed Betsy her room.

'Thank you, you're very kind,' the girl smiled gratefully, and Rhiannon felt a flush of guilt at her harsh feelings.

Minutes later she and Shane went to bed.

'I'm tired out,' she yawned, as she snuggled beneath the sheets.

He reached across and switched out the light. His hand was warm on her shoulder. 'Too tired?' he asked softly in the darkness.

'Yes.' She rolled away from him, deliberately perverse. She really wanted to feel his strong arms around her, holding her close, but she was angry because Betsy was sleeping only a room away. She heard him sigh, but within minutes he was fast asleep, breathing rhythmically, while she lay on her back, wide awake, until the streaks of dawn slashed the sky.

For the first few days Betsy was subdued. She wandered around the house like a wraith, showing little interest in anyone or anything. Shane's lighthearted attempts to explain how he arranged the songs were met with a blank face and uncomprehending silence. Even when Rhiannon took her into town and bought her some new clothes, she could only raise a tepid enthusiasm. She made no attempt to read newspapers, or listen to the radio, but spent most of her time idly drinking coffee and watching Mrs Jackson as she scurried around.

'Where's the swimming pool?' she asked one morning, out of the blue.

Shane's mouth twitched with amusement. 'No pool, I'm afraid, this isn't Hollywood.'

Betsy sank back into the doldrums.

But by the second week she had begun to venture out. She walked down into the village to buy pop magazines, and walked around the garden. She would sit on an old swing, suspended by ropes from the high branch of an oak tree, and chat with Alan Jackson as he cut the grass and swept up the fallen leaves. She never remained long in any one place. Every now and then she would return to the house, silently watching Shane at work in the music room, or leaning against the doorjamb while Rhiannon tidied the lounge. Rhiannon tried to keep calm, to tell herself that Betsy would soon leave, for her constant presence was irritating. It was impossible to find time alone with Shane. Any attempt at a serious discussion was out of the question, for Betsy would suddenly appear, pale and quiet, whenever they started to talk together, and sit quietly by, listening with avid curiosity to every word. It was impossible to decide whether her interest stemmed from a fascination with other people, or whether she was just plain nosey. Rhiannon decided it was the latter.

One morning she discovered her on the landing, staring into their bedroom.

'Can I come inside?' Betsy asked. Rhiannon fought back the desire to snap that it was really none of her business. She nodded her head briefly. The girl walked around the room, picking up ornaments, touching the lace coverlet.

'It's nice,' she said tepidly.

'Isn't it what you expected?'

Betsy shook her head, her ponytail swishing from side to side. 'I though you'd have had a special custom-built bed, very big, round or heart-shaped, with leopardskin rugs, and a mirrored ceiling.'

Rhiannon's temper faded and she giggled. 'I'm sorry to disappoint you, but we're very ordinary.'

'Yes,' replied Betsy, 'I think you are.' She followed Rhiannon downstairs. 'Don't you ever give parties, or have orgies?'

'We haven't done yet,' Rhiannon admitted, suppressing the desire to laugh as she went through to help Mrs Jackson with the vegetables for dinner. 'I suppose we might throw a housewarming one of these days, but we've not had time, we've been too busy.'

'All Shane does is play the piano—in bits. He doesn't even play one tune all the way through. Whenever I go into the music room to listen he's always playing short bursts. It's boring! He never listens to pop records on the stereo either.'

'We listened to Submission last night,' Rhiannon protested, slicing carrots.

'Only because Shane was being kind and asked me if I wanted to hear them. I could tell he wasn't interested himself.'

'But he's heard them a thousand times.'

'Where are his gold and platinum discs?' asked Betsy.

'In the safe, I imagine. He doesn't want them on show.'

'He should,' Betsy told her seriously. 'He should display them in the lounge, together with photographs of him shaking hands with Royalty.'

Shane walked into the kitchen. 'Want to come to the shops?' he asked Betsy with a smile. 'I've run out of manuscript paper and I need some cigars.'

'No, thank you,' she said politely, and he raised his eyebrows in surprise. So far, whenever he had moved, Betsy had moved too. She had been like his shadow, and Rhiannon had been impressed by his patience.

'No one ever knows I'm out with you, Shane Santiago of Submission,' Betsy muttered. 'You always wear those silly spectacles and that cap.'

'It's a disguise,' Shane spread his hands wide. 'If I go as I am I'd be recognised. Crowds would gather, and I'd have to sign autographs, and I can't waste time doing that when there's all the musical arrangements to be worked on. Besides, I don't like being stared at.'

'You go by yourself,' Betsy paused by the back door, 'and I'll go and talk to Alan.' She went out into the garden where Alan Jackson was pruning fruit bushes.

'I've been jilted!' Shane laughed delightedly, putting his arms around Rhiannon's slender waist and hugging her. Mrs Jackson wrapped the vegetable parings in an old newspaper and dropped them into the pedal bin.

'She likes my Alan,' she commented. 'She's a nice girl, but she needs something to do. It's not healthy for her to be hanging around here. I'll get Alan to talk to her, and try to find her a job.' She peered out of the window. 'There's a man out there,' she announced in surprise, 'talking to Betsy. It's that reporter chap, the one with the funny hair.'

'Buck Andrews!' Shane snorted, and strode out into the garden, Rhiannon at his shoulder. 'What are you doing here?' he asked sharply. Buck swivelled on the heels of his black patent leather boots to look up at him. He was bright in red leather trousers and a matching mohair jersey. A long football scarf in red and white stripes was coiled around his neck.

'Hi there, Shane,' he grinned, 'and how's my gorgeous girl?' He lifted Rhiannon's hand to his lips and kissed it loudly, while Betsy watched, wide-eyed and alert. Buck's appearance had revived her interest—here was a celebrity she'd heard about. Alan, snipping happily away in the background, was momentarily forgotten.

'I heard you'd set up a *ménage à trois*,' Buck twitched his nostrils. 'And I thought there might be a story in it somewhere—something on the lines of a new woman in Shane Santiago's bed.' He fluttered his eyelashes outrageously, and Rhiannon couldn't help laughing. Even Shane allowed himself a lukewarm smile, but then he glanced at Betsy.

'Cool it. Everyone's not as worldly as you.'

Betsy's face was deadly serious. 'I sleep in the spare bedroom,' she explained earnestly.

'I'm sure you do.' Buck arched a bleached brow and

looked her critically up and down, his expression indicating that she was doomed to sleep for ever in spare
bedrooms. 'You're not Shane's new lover?' he teased.
'You've not given Rhiannon the old heave-ho?'

Shane and Rhiannon looked on anxiously, unhappy
with the way he was baiting the young girl.

'No!' Betsy's plump face was indignant. 'Shane loves
Rhiannon, not me!'

'I never would have guessed,' Buck purred, stroking
the fringe of his long scarf. 'So I can't inform the world
that you and he are embarking on a torrid love affair?'

Betsy blushed bright pink. 'You're not nice!' She
thrust her chin in the air. 'I'm going to talk to Alan.'
She spun round and walked away, ignoring Buck's soft
laughter.

'Lay off her, Andrews,' Shane said quietly. There was
a warning in his words, not lightly given. 'She might not
be your idea of glamour, but she's basically a good kid.
Things haven't been easy for her.'

'She's the one you found suspended by her fingertips
from the thirtieth storey, isn't she?'

'It wasn't like that, as you well know. I don't want to
discuss it with Betsy around. Come into the house. I
can spare five minutes to put you straight on a few matters, and then you leave.'

The three of them went into the lounge. Buck sat on
the couch and casually crossed his legs, smoothing down
the red leather. 'To be straight with you, mates, I thought
there might be a human interest angle. I could do a
lovely spread on how you saved her from certain death,
invited her to live in your beautiful home, and helped
direct her towards a more meaningful life.' His forehead
puckered with derision.

'Get lost!' Shane snapped. 'That's a troubled girl out
there, even if she is a figure of fun to you. She'd never
be able to cope with the emotional stress if you splashed
her name all over the newspapers. She needs time to
find herself, to learn how to make friends and realise
she's a worthwhile human being. If you heaped publicity

on her, she'd be totally confused.'

Buck pulled down the corners of his mouth and grimaced.

'Keep away from her,' Shane said forcibly. 'I mean it.'

'Okay.' Buck examined his fingernails, then looked up suddenly, his eyes full of cunning. 'That marriage contract of yours is an intriguing proposition! I heard the full facts last night, so don't bother to deny it exists. Now that really would make one hell of a story!'

With one supple movement Shane leant forward and grabbed the reporter by the scarf around his neck. He lifted him until their faces were only inches apart, and Buck's feet barely scraped the carpet. Rhiannon gasped.

'What do you mean?' Shane snarled, his eyes glittering dangerously. Rhiannon felt cold fear grip the pit of her stomach.

'Don't choke me, mate!' Buck gave a strangled cough.

'I won't, so long as you tell me what you're talking about, what you're hoping to achieve, and what devious plan you have in mind.' With a snort of disgust Shane released his grip, and Buck fell back onto the couch. There were angry red marks at his throat where the scarf had bitten into his flesh, and he rubbed at them tenderly, and stretched his neck, as if trying to determine whether or not there were any broken bones. Shane bent over him menacingly. 'Tell me all you know, Andrews, but any funny business, and I'll not just bruise your neck, I'll break it!' He looked as though he meant it. He sat heavily on the arm of Rhiannon's chair and glared at the reporter, his eyes like flint.

Buck swallowed a few times then summoned up a measure of retaliation. 'I know you both signed a marriage contract—I heard the details from a lady friend of mine. We happened to be exchanging confidences in very intimate surroundings last night.'

'I can imagine,' Shane snapped. 'Spare us the descriptive passages.'

'She informed me that you issued an ultimatum and Rhiannon complied. She said only a handful of people know of the contract, and that it expires after a year.'

'It was Kim,' Rhiannon decided flatly.

Buck gave a nod. 'We're knocking around together. I can be very persuasive when I try. I've always suspected there was something offbeat about your relationship, so I worked on Kim. She was very proud of the fact that the scheme was her idea, and she told me the full story.'

'In complete and utter confidence, of course!' Shane growled.

'Of course. I shan't say a word, Scout's honour.' Buck's tone was flippantly threatening.

'How do you know Kim was telling the truth?' Rhiannon asked, hoping, in vain, to retrieve the situation.

'She was. And don't imagine I couldn't obtain a copy of that contract if I tried. Everyone has their price. Even Eddie Beagle might spill the beans if he was offered sufficient inducement, and think of the publicity! Submission could trade for years on a touch of intrigue like that.'

'You won't publish the story, will you?' Rhiannon asked, her heart fluttering like a frightened, captive bird. 'It would be humiliating, and it's not only us who would suffer.'

Buck glanced at her anxious face. 'I don't give a damn if Shane suffers,' he retorted, exchanging a belligerent look with him, 'but I must admit I care about you. I don't want to cause you unhappiness. I'll make a deal. I promise not to write anything, not even a whisper, on one condition.'

'And that is?' Shane barked.

'You give me the inside information about the contract, to satisfy my curiosity. I'm not a journalist for nothing. It's fascinating to learn how people tick.'

'No!'

'Then threaten me all you like, but I'll publish.'

There was a long, dangerous silence. Rhiannon put

her hand on Shane's arm. He looked at her, then gave a shrug of resignation.

'We'll tell you,' Rhiannon said gently.

Buck leaned forward, immediately alert and professional. 'You've been married nearly five months, but in seven months' time you split—right?'

'Right,' snapped Shane, to Rhiannon's utter astonishment. Why didn't he defuse Buck's threat by telling him their marriage was for real?

'It's merely a façade?' probed Buck. 'You don't really love each other?'

'Right,' Shane repeated. Rhiannon bent her head and stared at her wedding ring, her mind growing slowly numb as Shane denied their love. She sat in a daze as Buck continued his questions, all in the same vein, all circling around their relationship.

'So it's a business arrangement?'

'Just a business arrangement,' Shane confirmed matter-of-factly, rubbing the black curls at the nape of his neck. Rhiannon swallowed hard. She had imagined that when he had spoken of discussing the future and setting things right, he had meant he wanted them to remain together in the future, but she had been wrong. She furiously backtracked over his words and realised he had never actually committed himself. She stared miserably at the golden band. All he had wanted to do was bring his true feelings out into the open and clear the way for ending their relationship without making it too painful for her. Her eyes brimmed with tears, and she stood up briskly. 'I'll go and talk to Betsy,' she said, walking hurriedly from the room.

Blindly she strode towards a far corner of the garden and laid her forehead against the trunk of the oak tree as scorching tears tumbled down her cheeks. What a fool she'd been! Because their life and lovemaking together was good she had presumed Shane had really meant it when he had said he loved her. She had deliberately thrust aside the memory of his other relationships, but doubtless he had convinced other women too, that he had loved them. And she was no different, except that with her he had had double value. In addition to furnishing his bed, she had also furnished his home. Now he would be able to live comfortably in it, with whomever he pleased. She wiped away the tears with the back of her hand, and looked around in agitation. She had forgotten about Betsy and Alan, but the garden was deserted. They were nowhere to be seen.

Quietly she slipped upstairs to the bedroom and bathed her face. The sound of the men's voices drifted up, and eventually she heard Buck shout goodbye and drive away. A few moments later Shane called up the stairs that he was going out to buy his manuscript paper and cigars. Rhiannon was relieved he hadn't seen her tear-stained face, and by the time he returned, in time for dinner, she was carefully in control of the violent emotions which simmered precariously below the surface of her apparent composure. Betsy appeared again and ate her meal with unusual gusto. Then she rocked back on her chair and announced she was going to the cinema and would be back around eleven.

'Thank goodness,' Shane grinned, when Betsy had departed. 'Our first evening alone in what seems like ages!' He stretched out on the couch. 'Perhaps we can indulge in a little civilised conversation, instead of listening to pop records or watching television.'

'I'm going to bed,' Rhiannon told him carefully. 'I have a bad headache, the light hurts my eyes.'

He was immediately sympathetic. 'Do you want a cup of tea, or some aspirins?'

'Just leave me alone,' she said abruptly. 'I'll be fine.'

She was asleep when Shane went up to bed.

Betsy stirred her spoon around and around in her cup of breakfast coffee the next morning. 'I have something to tell you,' she announced brightly. 'I'm leaving, today, in half an hour.' Shane and Rhiannon shared a glance of surprise.

'I've found a job in the village—I shall be caring for

two little girls. Their parents are friends of Alan's, and I shall live in their house. I'll have my own room. Mrs Jackson can tell you more about it when she arrives.'

'Isn't this very sudden?' Shane asked cautiously. 'Are you sure it's what you want?'

'I'm sure.' Betsy pushed at the nosepiece of her spectacles. 'Alan and I have been planning it for a few days, and also,' she blushed, 'we're going steady.'

'After a week?' Shane raised an eyebrow.

'Yes.' The girl threw him a scornful glance. 'He's lots of fun. He makes me laugh. He enjoys the things I like—pop music and the cinema.' She replaced the spoon in her saucer. 'You've both been very kind, but really it's a bit quiet for me here. Nothing exciting ever happens, it's not what I imagined.'

'You can't please all the people all the time,' Shane remarked drily. 'Personally *I* find life particularly exciting in this part of the world.' He flashed a quick look at Rhiannon, who ignored the sensual meaning to his words. 'But you must do what you wish. When you're ready I'll drive you to your new home.'

'Thanks.' Betsy gave him a wide smile and jumped up gaily. 'I've put my things in a couple of carrier bags. Alan's going to come with me to my parent's house next weekend, and I can collect all my belongings from there.' She ran upstairs, humming happily to herself. In a few minutes she was down again, stood by the front door and giving Rhiannon a quick hug of farewell. She climbed eagerly into the car beside Shane, her brown paper carrier bags slung on the back seat, and waved frantically as they drove away.

When Mrs Jackson arrived Rhiannon heard the full story.

'Betsy's ever so good with children—they just adore her,' Mrs Jackson enthused. 'Alan's friends took to her straight away. The wife wants to go back to work and she needs someone who really cares about children. Alan will keep an eye on Betsy, too, so she'll come to no harm. She's beginning to find her feet, you can see that already. A touch more confidence is all she needs.'

When Shane returned he, too, had to hear the full details of Betsy's new job.

'I bet that's the last we'll see of her,' he grinned, his hands in his pockets as he lounged against the door frame of the music room. 'She thinks Alan is a darn sight more exciting than I am.'

'Perhaps he is,' Rhiannon said tartly, brushing past him.

'What do you mean by that?' Shane grabbed her upper arm. 'Aren't I the most exciting man you've ever known?' he teased, bending to kiss her mouth, but Rhiannon moved away.

'Hadn't you better start work? You've lost an hour already by delivering Betsy.'

He looked at her thoughtfully, narrowing his blue eyes. 'I suppose so. I must have it finished by the end of the week.'

He worked in the music room for the rest of the day. Rhiannon was uneasy. She baked some fruit pies for the freezer, did some shopping, and worked in the garden for a while. When Mrs Jackson had departed she walked around the house, trailing her fingers fondly over the furnishings she and Shane had chosen. She could hear the muted sound of the piano, but she felt isolated and trapped. She was already deeply in love with Shane, but how much worse would she feel at the end of the marriage contract when he walked away? Her stomach churned in despair. She didn't know how she could continue living with him, and yet how could she live without him? She gave a sigh and automatically began to prepare dinner. She set the table in the dining alcove and then looked out of the kitchen window, her thoughts far away.

If only her problems could be resolved as easily as Betsy's! Shane had handled that situation so well. He had opened Betsy's eyes, made her realise she was living in a dream world, and set her feet firmly back on the path to reality. Rhiannon felt an irrational stab of jealousy. He had *cared* about Betsy. He had been so kind, so patient, never forcing the issue, allowing the girl to work out her insecurities in her own way. But Betsy's life was simple, that was the difference. She wasn't living inside the goldfish bowl of fame, with its accompanying strains and pressures. Rhiannon closed her eyes. Why couldn't *she* have an uncomplicated existence? All she really desired was a happy marriage, a couple of children, and a devoted husband—Shane. He could work the same magic for her as he had done for Betsy. If he wanted to. But he didn't.

His voice startled her from her reveries. 'A very successful day,' he reported with a grin. 'The arrangements will be finished in good time, at this rate. Would you like a drink before dinner?'

'I'll have a sherry, please—dry.'

The full skirt of her soft coral jersey dress swirled around her legs as she walked through to the lounge. She sat on the couch and looked deep into the fire. Shane appeared and handed the sherry glass to her. He was drinking whisky and water. He raised his glass to hers. 'We must celebrate. At last we've persuaded Betsy that the grass really is greener on her side of the fence, and we also appear to have defused the explosive Buck Andrews.'

'And now we can sit back calmly for the next seven months and wait for the end of the contract when we part, as you told Buck.' Rhiannon's voice was hard as a bubble of anger and dismay rose inside her at Shane's maddening complacency.

He put down his tumbler and sat beside her. 'We don't have to sit and wait. I can think of at least one exciting way to pass the time.' His voice was low and vibrant, and despite her annoyance Rhiannon felt her skin begin to tingle. He put out an index finger and ran it along the curve of her cheekbone. But when he bent forward as if to kiss her she rounded on him, her eyes glittering. 'I'm just another woman for you to seduce, aren't I?'

'No, you're not.' His reply was indignant. 'You're my wife. I love you.'

'You say that to keep me sweet, to make sure you get your legalised sex. You'll pretend you love me until the contract expires and then you'll just walk away. You said you were eager for it to finish.'

Shane shook his dark head. 'I'm eager to leave Submission, *not you*. I've never had to pretend about what I feel for you. I do love you—that's the truth, I've told you often enough. And it's not a twelve-month feeling. I've never said I wanted to walk away from you at the end. It's you who are so adamant about the contract and our relationship being a temporary arrangement.'

'*Me?*'

'Whenever I speak about the future, you're always so quick to remind me that there isn't any, for us.' He took a swift gulp from his glass.

'But you don't care, you've never spoken about our future,' Rhiannon accused, breathing rapidly.

'Of course I care!'

'When you spoke to Buck you agreed our marriage was a façade, you told him we didn't love each other.'

'I lied.' Shane's eyes darkened, and he rubbed at a nerve which was flickering in his cheek. 'I had no intention of baring my soul to him, before we'd even discussed the future properly ourselves. What happens between you and me is private. I refuse to reveal my intimate feelings to a newspaper reporter. He was so eager to hear all about it, I was damned if I was going to tell *him* the truth!' He paused. 'But you were right about me not committing myself—the future is your decision, not mine.'

'No, it's not,' she blurted. 'You've made all the decisions concerning us so far, why change now? Tell me what you want to do!' There was a note of desperation in her plea.

'Don't you understand, my darling,' gently he took hold of her hand, 'that's what's been wrong all along. I've made too many decisions in our relationship. I more or less trapped you into marrying me, and then I refused to allow us to function on a platonic level. You never had time to make up your own mind, I was always steering you along where *I* wanted to go. This time it's different. I shall never force you into anything, ever again.' He looked at her beneath his dark lashes, 'I decided some time ago that I wouldn't influence your future in any way, that's why I deliberately kept quiet. What I want isn't important any more; it's what you want that matters. You must make up your own mind.' He let go her hand and stood up abruptly. 'It would be better if I went away. It would give you time to breathe, time to decide what you really want to do.' He swallowed down the remains of his drink. 'It's no use pretending I can live here and not make love to you, and if I do the physical side will cloud the issue.'

Rhiannon gazed at him thoughtfully. 'But there won't be any insistent fans or pressure of publicity after the end of the contract. You'll be able to live here in peace, you won't need me then.'

Shane drew a deep breath and sat heavily down beside her.

'The fans were never important. Oh, they were irritating, but they were an excuse. All I wanted, at the beginning, was you in my bed. I didn't care if I had to marry you to get you there. I knew you'd never sleep with me on a casual basis, although I had tried to persuade you. I was surrounded by women who would have done anything for me, but you, the only one I wanted, kept her distance. I'll be honest, initially you were intended to be another love affair, nothing more, for a year. I thought you'd had some experience, and could handle a temporary relationship. That's why I went berserk when you told me you were a virgin. It altered the whole scenario. You ceased to be a casual tumble in the hay. You were a real woman, someone who cared about close relationships. Then, to confuse matters, I realised I was beginning to fall in love with you. I'd never felt like that before,' he gave a shamefaced smile. 'I know

I've had so-called love affairs but they were one-dimensional—sex and little else. I suddenly discovered that in addition to being my wife and my lover, you were my friend. We relate on all kinds of levels, we laugh at the same things, we have the same interests.' He turned away. 'But the future is your decision. I'm cutting down on being a male chauvinist from now on. If you want to finish our marriage when the contract ends, so be it. Or if you want to opt out now—tomorrow—next week— I'll understand. I won't like it, but I'll understand. You were forced into this situation, and I wouldn't blame you for getting out as quickly as you can. I want you to have the house.' He swept a glance around the lounge. 'It's your creation. It has your style, your personality. I couldn't bear to live here without you. It's only fair you should have some compensation for my selfishness.'

Rhiannon looked at him for a long moment, then she put out a hand and touched his cheek. 'I love you,' she said, sliding her fingertips down to trace the outline of his mouth. Shane kissed her fingers. 'My decision was made a long time ago,' she continued, a little smile playing on her lips. 'I'll only accept the house as long as the pianist comes with it!'

Shane laughed. He wrapped his arms around her and held her so tightly against his chest she could feel the heavy beat of his heart.

'For ever?' he asked.

'For ever,' said Rhiannon.

CHAPTER NINE

THEY ate dinner late that evening, and if the steak was a little charred around the edges neither of them noticed.

'Why don't we visit the Philippines while we're on the Far East tour?' Rhiannon suggested later as they sat lazily before a blazing fire, replete with food and love. 'Perhaps you could trace your father's family.'

Shane put his arm around her. 'I've always felt the urge to go,' he admitted, 'but now that everything has turned out so perfectly here I'm loath to disturb it. Supposing it really did feel like home to me and I wanted to live there, would you mind? Would you be happy to live abroad?'

'I'd be fine,' she assured him quickly, brushing aside a sudden quiver of dismay. 'I think it's important for you to learn more about your background. You'll never be completely settled until you do.'

'Perhaps you're right,' he frowned. 'I've always felt torn two ways. My English blood wants to put down roots here, but I've always had that touch of restlessness. I'd like to resolve my feelings about my Filipino ancestry. Who knows, I might discover it's my natural home after all, or perhaps it won't mean a thing.' He hugged her to him. 'Thank you for understanding.'

Rhiannon felt a fraud. If she was honest, she didn't really want him to go. She didn't want to meet his Filipino family who would share his dark good looks and volatile moods. She was terrified that they would entice him away into their foreign world. Perhaps they would force a wedge between the East and the West in him—between him and her. And yet she knew that his feelings of insecurity were caused by his erratic childhood. If he could solve the mystery surrounding his father, he would be able to come to terms with his background and throw off the wanderlust which plagued him.

'It'll be exciting to discover long-lost relatives,' he smiled, already planning the visit in his mind. Rhiannon nibbled thoughtfully at the tip of her thumb nail, and decided that although a visit to the Philippines was necessary for his happiness, it could possibly be disastrous for hers. But it was a chance she was compelled to take. To shut her eyes to his needs would be quite wrong. And if he did want to settle there, then at least she would be with him.

'We'll visit my mother next weekend,' Shane continued. 'When she knows we're going perhaps she'll open up about my father.' He raised his brows laconically. 'Though I doubt it.'

His mother and his stepfather Ernest lived in the leafy suburbs of a Kent market town. Mrs Santiago had settled there on her return to England, and her home was her delight, her refuge, her nest. She had welcomed Rhiannon into the family with relief, having long disapproved of her son's quicksilver path through a stream of women, and she had hoped that because he had finally committed himself to marriage his restless urge would disappear.

After a tasty lunch of roast beef, Yorkshire pudding and all the trimmings, they moved out into the garden room for coffee and liqueurs. The autumn day was sunny, and Ernest opened wide the French windows to allow a soft breeze to circulate.

'Rhiannon and I are going to Manila to trace Dad's family,' Shane announced casually, sipping his brandy.

His mother's face turned ashen and she gripped the arms of her chair. 'You mustn't go,' she said fiercely, leaning forward. 'There's absolutely no point. You'd never find them.'

'For heaven's sake, Mother,' he protested with a laugh, 'I know it's years since there's been any communication, but we do have my grandparents' address. I intend to make enquiries there. The whole family can't have disappeared from the face of the earth!'

'The last I heard only your grandfather was alive, but he's probably dead by now,' she faltered.

'There must be other relations,' Shane insisted.

'*No.*'

'How can you be sure? You've never been to Manila. Dad must have had other relations, cousins perhaps, they would still be alive. I could trace them.'

'There must be millions of Santiagos in the Philippines. It's a sheer waste of time. You're not to go, Shane.'

They stared at each other for a long moment. Mrs Santiago was a faded English rose, with her pink and white complexion, and greying blonde hair. Shane's sultry good looks and golden skin could be attributed only to his father.

'We're going,' he said doggedly. 'If we're unlucky, nothing is wasted, we still get to see the country.' He shrugged his wide shoulders. 'It's something I must do. It's not so unusual to be interested in one's ancestry, plenty of people are. I want to visit Dad's home and find out more about him. I'm sure the police or some Government office would be able to help me.'

'You mustn't go!' His mother's voice rose shrilly, and Ernest put out a hand to calm her. 'I mean it—don't interfere.'

'Why not?'

'I can't tell you,' she sighed. 'I'm sorry, but I can't.'

'*We're going to the Philippines.*'

His mother looked around at Rhiannon in desperation. 'Stop him!' she pleaded, twisting her fingers in her lap.

Rhiannon shook her head. 'I don't want to.'

'There you are, mother,' Shane smiled, 'Rhiannon's happy that we should go, so tell me why you think we shouldn't.'

His mother licked her lips nervously. 'All right. I've kept this a secret for many years. Your father made me swear never to tell, but I suppose now that he's dead. . . .' Her voice trailed away. All eyes were upon her. She sat up straight in her chair, and cleared her throat.

'As you know, your father was born in England. *His* father was a sailor who married an English girl. When your father was in his teens the family went to live in Manila. He found it difficult to adjust to the East, after being brought up in England, and being hot-tempered, like you, he had a pretty rough time.' She glanced at her son. 'He clung to his Western ideas, and antagonised the neighbourhood youths. He was also devoted to his piano. You must understand that the district they lived in was working class. People didn't have money to spare for such fripperies as pianos, but your father was gifted, and his parents made sacrifices to allow him to continue his music. There he was, the neighbours thought, wasting his time playing the piano all day. It wasn't something they could understand. So your father was an outcast for two reasons—he had mixed blood, and he was a musician. Like you, Shane, he wasn't prepared to compromise. He was proud.' Mrs Santiago paused and everyone waited, then she swallowed hard. 'He wouldn't conform to the Filipino way of life and he wouldn't give up his beloved music, so he had to fight. And that's what he did. He fought physically. When the local youths taunted him he'd retaliate and fists would fly, but he was tall and strongly made, and he won enough fights for them to accord him a measure of respect. They began to leave him alone, apart from one young man, the son of a local politician. He resented your father, speaking fluent English and playing classical piano, and one night he waited in the dark for him. They had a fight. Your father hit him, and he fell backwards, against a wall. When your father heard his skull crack he knew he'd killed him.' Her voice faded. Everyone strained forward to hear the end of the tale. A lone plane droned overhead unnoticed.

'He left Manila the next day. The politician was a shady character, on the criminal fringe. He would have arranged for your father to be killed. He knew he could never return to the Philippines, and for the rest of his life he lived in fear of being discovered and dragged back there.'

'So that's why we were constantly on the move—we were fugitives!' Shane leant back in his chair and rubbed his jaw, his eyes hooded.

Mrs Santiago nodded sadly. 'He told me the full story before we were married. It's ironical, I thought it was terribly romantic. I never realised what it would be like, spending my life continually running away. My parents didn't want me to marry your father. They threatened to disown me, but their opposition made me all the more determined, and there were terrible scenes. But he was tall, dark and handsome, and the thought of him fighting for his way of life added that extra zest. I was young and foolish then.' She lowered her eyes. 'In the end your father became obsessed with the idea he was being hounded, and it ruined our marriage. It was a relief when he died and I could return to England, for ever.' She turned to Shane and took hold of his hand. 'Please don't go!'

'All this happened forty-odd years ago, Mother,' he said reasonably. 'There's no danger now.'

'Filipinos are hot-blooded people, and the politician's family might still hold a grudge. If you start raking over the past they could decide to take revenge.'

Shane laughed. 'What, after all this time? Nonsense! In any case, I'm perfectly capable of looking after myself, and Rhiannon.'

Mrs Santiago looked doubtful.

Shane put his hands together in a steeple. 'Wouldn't Buck Andrews be delighted to know I'm the son of a murderer?' he said grimly.

'Goodbye, Submission—Come Back Soon—We Love You.'

The red and white banner bucked and plunged in the wind. The airport's viewing deck was thronged with fans who had been gathering for hours to bid farewell. To the uninitiated it seemed a worthless exercise. At best, all they could possibly see was a distant face in the porthole of a plane, but for the devoted fans it was enough to be present to wave goodbye as Submission flew off to Singapore at the start of their Far Eastern tour.

Outside the departure hall more crowds, four and five deep, lined both sides of the road. A polished limousine turned the corner on the final approach to the entrance, and the fans cheered wildly, pushing and straining against the barriers. Anxious policemen tried in vain to instil an aura of calm, and kept their fingers crossed that the metal restraining rails would hold. The limousine bearing Tony and David pulled to a halt. A policeman opened the door, and the two young men got out, grinning and waving. As they strode rapidly forward arms reached out from either side of the barriers, notes were flung before them, a girl fainted, roses were pushed into their hands, there were shouts and cheers, a barrage of smiling faces, and then they were clear, safe in the airport building.

As another limousine negotiated the corner, interest switched. Rhiannon sat close beside Shane in the rear seat, and the crowd bayed its satisfaction.

'Look at that mob!' Shane muttered, tugging irritably at the collar of his black suede jacket, which he wore over a black shirt and trousers. His sultry good looks were accentuated by the unrelenting sombreness of his clothes. Eddie turned from the front seat to trot out instructions.

'You know the form—the minute the car stops make a run for it. There's a path cleared between the crowds, and once you're through the entrance there'll be airport staff to direct you to a private lounge. Don't stop whatever happens—keep moving.'

Shane gave a terse nod, and gripped Rhiannon's hand. There was a moment of hesitation, then the chauffeur accelerated, and with a squeal of tyres braked abruptly before the entrance. The door was flung open and Shane leapt out, pulling Rhiannon with him.

'Shane, Shane!' the girls yelled. For an instant his eyes swept over them, then he dragged Rhiannon quickly behind him into the narrow gap. Instantly they were awash in a sea of humanity. It was claustrophobic and deafening. Everyone was shouting, and a hundred pairs of eyes watched them avidly. A jumble of tentacles reached out to grab them, tear them apart. Rhiannon was frightened. Her heart raced as she felt an alien hand catch at the sleeve of her white linen suit. It tightened its grip, and she was trapped, torn between Shane, a step ahead, and pulling her forward, and the unrelenting claw restraining her from behind. She struggled desperately to free herself. Shane half turned, then his strong arm was around her shoulders. He forced her forwards until the hand was compelled to release its grip, and she was running beside him through pale tiled corridors to the haven of the lounge.

'Thank God!' Shane released a gasp of relief as they leant breathlessly against the wall, panting heavily. 'That's one part of fame I shall be delighted to leave behind.'

Despite the comfort of the first class cabin, the flight to Singapore was long and boring. For sixteen hours they flew across the continents, with only an hour's transit stop on the desert sands of Bahrein. Rhiannon dozed fitfully, her slumber disturbed by fleeting images of Shane's Filipino relatives, of them welcoming him, but pushing her aside. *He* might belong in the East, but she knew she never would. Although she loved to travel, she was always happy to return home to the United Kingdom. For a terrifying instant she had a vision of her marriage disintegrating as his mother's had done before, then she shook her head. The long journey was making her morbid. In her distress she rubbed Shane's warm, dry palm, as he lay back beside her. He opened his eyes for a moment, and grinned sleepily before closing them again. She studied the wide brow that she loved so much, his fine, straight nose, the dark lashes on his cheek, and the cleft in his chin. His jaw was dark with stubble and his hair curled below his collar. It was growing long again, and Eddie had instructed he was not to cut it until he finally left Submission.

After performing before record-breaking crowds at Singapore's National Stadium, Submission flew on to Jakarta, Kuala Lumpur and Bangkok, where they were received with equal delight. Their image had never been soiled by rumours of drug-taking or violence, and the authorities were pleased to welcome them. The Asian fans were not as demanding as those back home, and they were able to move around easily. The days between concerts were relaxed, and they were able to see the sights and sunbathe on the beaches.

'Thanks for keeping the paperwork in order, Rhi,' Eddie smiled when they came to part at the end of the tour. Everyone was taking a well-earned rest. Some were flying on to the Seychelles or Hawaii before meeting up again in England in a month's time.

'My pleasure! It wasn't too hectic.'

'How about coming with us on our American tour next spring? Shane won't be with us, but,' he winked, 'we'll always have room for you.'

'Like hell!' Shane intervened happily. 'Chances are she'll be pregnant by then.'

Or living in the Philippines, Rhiannon thought wryly.

The airport in Manila was hot, airless and crowded. They had to fight their way through the crush of travellers to reach the exit, and then fight again to find a place near the taxi stand.

'It's not like England, is it?' Rhiannon clutched her travel bag as she stared about her. There was no orderly queue. Instead hurrying travellers milled around, laughing and shouting to each other in a strange tongue, pushing and jostling, gesticulating and arguing. Every time an empty taxi appeared there was one almighty scramble, when toes were stood on, tempers frayed and luggage lost. They waited patiently, somewhat stunned by the commotion swirling about them, but when an interloper forced his way outrageously to the head of the straggling queue and into the next taxi, Shane had had enough.

'*Ours!*' he barked to all and sundry as the next free taxi arrived, and although the crowds didn't understand English, his message came across loud and clear. His height and natural air of authority made him a force to be reckoned with, and for once everyone hung back while he shepherded Rhiannon forward, and gave the address of their hotel to the driver.

'What language is it?' Rhiannon asked as, with a great deal of noisy banter, the driver pulled away from the airport building.

'Tagalog.'

'Did you learn any from your father?'

'Not a chance!' Shane grimaced. 'Anything Filipino was taboo.'

She gazed out of the taxi with wide interested eyes. There seemed to be utter confusion and much sounding of horns, but everything kept moving.

'Those look like fun,' she laughed, pointing to a bevy of gaily painted jeeps, collecting passengers from street corners. Each vehicle had coloured streamers, red, yellow, blue and green, tied to radio aerials on either side of the windscreen. The bonnets were crowded with round driving mirrors and silver statuettes of horses which glittered in the tropical sun.

'Those are jeepneys. That's something Dad *did* tell me about. The original ones were left behind by the Americans at the end of World War Two,' Shane explained. 'The locals converted them, and gradually they've become a form of public transport. The fares are very cheap. The drivers are very proud of their vehicles, and each year there are fierce competitions to decide which one is the best decorated.'

As they drew alongside the crowded jeepneys they heard the blast of pop music. There were stacks of cassette tapes beneath the dashboards, and the sides of the vehicles were covered with painted slogans—some amusing, some romantic. Rhiannon studied the people thoughtfully. 'You don't look so Filipino, after all—the people are darker-skinned. You're just a watered-down version.'

He raised his brows and laughed, 'There are some stunning-looking girls,' he teased.

'And some good-looking men,' she retorted with spirit. 'Guys like you are ten a penny here!'

The hotel was a luxurious, shining white wedding cake of a building overlooking Manila Bay. A smiling boy, who looked no more than twelve, directed them to their room. He was smart in his dark green uniform, with a row of gold buttons down his jacket, and a neat pillbox hat. He grinned as Shane tipped him, and when he had departed they stood together at the window, watching the traffic speeding along Roxas Boulevard below them. The sun was setting, and the water of the bay reflected the soft colours of the evening sky—delicate pink, dove grey and soft blue.

'Mustn't waste time,' Shane declared, abandoning the beauty of the sunset. He lifted the telephone book on to the desk and began searching through the pages. Rhiannon sighed at his enthusiasm and sat down wearily on the bed. It had been a long day. They had been awake at dawn and travelling ever since.

'You look tired,' said Shane. 'Have a rest, while I make a start with my enquiries.' He continued leafing through the book. 'My mother was right, there *are* thousands of Santiagos. I'll go down to reception and ask if they have a street map.'

After he had gone Rhiannon lay down on the bed and was soon asleep. It was dark when he returned and woke her. He was exultant, and she had to bite back her annoyance. She knew she was being unfair, but she had secretly been hoping he wouldn't be able to trace his family and would abandon the search. But she'd forgotten his determination. He didn't give up easily, she thought, remembering the circumstances of their marriage.

'The address I had was for a building which was demolished years ago,' he told her. 'However, the girl on reception was very helpful.'

'And pretty?'

'I suppose she was. She telephoned the housing authority for me and eventually discovered where the families were rehoused. The new address didn't appear on any map, but one of the hotel porters lives in the area, and after a great deal of confusion and broken English he drew a sketch map. The street is about a thirty-minute drive from here, so I hired a taxi and went to have a look.'

Rhiannon's face fell. 'You promised to take me.'

'Don't worry, I will,' he smiled at her crestfallen face. 'In the dark it was rather forbidding. In any case I couldn't see any street names, so I had the taxi drive around for a while and then came back. We'll go first thing in the morning. At least I know the area in which to begin making enquiries.' He took her in his arms and rubbed his cheek against hers. 'And then I'll discover my Filipino family,' he said happily.

The following morning he awoke early, and had Rhiannon dressed, breakfasted and installed in a taxi outside the hotel before nine o'clock. The taxi driver was a surly man, but he appeared to understand some English, and after brandishing the sketch map beneath his nose they set off. Soon they had left the expensive hotels and chic stores of the tourist belt far behind. The broad streets narrowed, gradually turning into rough, uneven thoroughfares, lined with dilapidated shops and houses.

Rhiannon eyed the tumbledown buildings apprehensively, and caught hold of Shane's arm. 'I don't like it here,' she said, biting her lip. 'It looks dangerous. The neighbourhood is so poor, we're going to stand out like a sore thumb—obvious tourists. We'll be a target for pickpockets and thieves.'

He nodded grimly. 'I hoped it would look better in the daylight, but it doesn't. Perhaps I have the wrong address. You stay in the taxi while I make enquiries. I'll come and fetch you if I have any luck. It would certainly be wise to keep a low profile. I'll leave my wallet with you.' He handed it over and she tucked it away in her shoulder bag. The taxi stopped, and the driver gesticulated brusquely. They gazed out at a four-storey building, presumably tenements, which was in an advanced state of decay. The painted walls were black with grime, and many of the windows were broken. Dejected clumps of grass sprouted hopelessly among the debris. There was a short flight of broken stone steps which led to a half open door.

'Are you sure?' Shane asked the taxi driver, frowning at the unsavoury appearance of the building.

The man punched his finger at the sketch map and nodded vigorously. 'This house, this house,' he grumbled.

'I suppose he's right.' Shane was disappointed. 'I'll see what I can discover.' He climbed from the taxi and turned to the driver. 'Stay here,' he said firmly. The man gave a curt nod. 'Don't leave the taxi on any account, Rhi—I don't want you in danger. I won't be long.' He glanced worriedly over his shoulder at a gang of youths who were idly watching them from the street corner. 'Don't forget, stay in the taxi.'

She nodded. The last thing she intended to do was wander around alone in such a rough area. She watched Shane brace his shoulders and stride into the building.

The taxi driver was staring at her through his mirror, and hastily she averted her eyes and looked out of the window. The youths were pointing at the taxi and laughing. Rhiannon trembled. As the minutes passed she became uncomfortably aware of the fact that she was a foreigner in a strange land, unable to speak the language and extremely vulnerable. The atmosphere was menacing, and a shiver of fright trickled down her spine.

Nervously she plucked at her hair.

Suddenly the taxi driver twisted round in his seat to peer at her, 'Money,' he said harshly, pointing to the leather shoulder bag. She gasped. He must have seen Shane pass her his wallet.

'Later,' she said, her voice coming out in a squeak. 'At hotel.'

The man would not, or could not, understand. He shook his head and thrust a muscular arm between the seats to gesture again roughly at the bag.

'No,' she said again, shaking her head, 'at hotel.'

The man muttered darkly beneath his breath, and turned forward, slapping at the black plastic steering wheel in annoyance. Rhiannon looked down, avoiding his hard eyes which were again examining her through the mirror. She wished Shane would hurry. He'd been gone ten minutes already.

'Money now,' the driver demanded, turning again so that his face was close to hers. He had square, yellowish teeth, and his stale breath flooded her nostrils. She leant back from him. He said something loud and angry, which she did not understand.

'Money *now*,' he said again, waving his fist. She pointed out of the window at the tenements, indicating that Shane would soon return, but the taxi driver paid no attention. Instead he made a lunge for her bag. She scrambled across the seat away from him, opened the wallet and thrust two notes into his hand. She had no idea of their value, but she was prepared to pay anything to pacify him. He grabbed the notes and thrust them into the pocket of his shirt.

'Out!' he rasped, stretching across her, and opening the rear door. Rhiannon shook her head wildly. She was almost in tears. He refused to understand that Shane would soon return. Then he reached over and began pushing her from the taxi, his hands impatient and unyielding.

There was a loud guffaw from the group of youths on the corner, who were watching the drama with great amusement. Rhiannon had no alternative but to stagger from the car on to the pavement. With one fluid movement the driver slammed shut the door, gunned the engine, and drove away with an angry backward glance and a squeal of tyres.

She stood alone on the broken paving slabs and looked about her, wondering what to do. To her horror, one of the youths detached himself from the group and began walking across the stretch of waste land towards her. His mates were shouting out what sounded like instructions, and there was a great deal of sniggering. Her heart froze with fear. She clutched at her bag and eyed the approaching youth with trepidation. He was short and muscular, and he swaggered insolently towards her, flexing his shoulders. In a moment of panic Rhiannon decided it would be safer to go into the tenement and find Shane. With a hurried glance over her shoulder she ran forward, stumbling over the rubble on the steps. The youth quickened his pace, and there was a hoot of laughter from his friends. She ran into the building, and slammed the door shut behind her.

The hallway was gloomy. A shaft of weak light came from a dirty skylight high in the roof, and a single illuminated electric bulb hung nakedly on a twisted black wire. Two doors led from the hallway, both tightly closed. Rhiannon peered up the stairs and saw more doors on the upper stories, again all shut. Scabs of old paint hung from the dirty walls and the bare floor was littered with rusted cans and old newspapers. There was a dank smell which she couldn't identify.

Suddenly the front door creaked and began to swing slowly open. Rapidly she slammed it shut, and then realised, with a tremor of fear, that the lock was broken. The door moved again, and she heard a low, sinister chuckle. She pushed her full weight against it.

'Shane!' she shouted, but it was too late. With one strong movement the youth jolted the door open and grabbed her, a rough, dirty hand across her mouth. Rhiannon almost gagged. Her skin crawled at his touch.

He chuckled again as she struggled, his grip firm and
relentless. Then, slowly, he slid his other hand across
her chest. She fought desperately, trying to drag his
hands from her. She kicked at his shins, but he never
flinched. He breathed into her ear, and whispered
something which she knew had to be obscene. His lank,
dirty hair brushed her cheek. His fingers caught at the
bodice of her floral dress, and he gurgled as slowly he
began forcing the flimsy material aside. She fought desperately, the cold sweat of fear on her forehead. She
twisted and turned in his arms, trying to release the grip
of the fist across her mouth, the hand sliding over her
rib cage.

Suddenly there was the sound of footsteps on the
stairs, and Shane flew down them, roaring with anger.
He dragged the young man from her and hit him in the
stomach. Her assailant staggered back, groaning, then
he gave a gulp and charged at Shane. They struggled
together, while Rhiannon watched in horror, gasping
for breath. The fight was fast and furious. Then Shane
forced the youth back against the stairs. His fist flashed
out and his opponent fell back, blood trickling from the
side of his mouth. The youth sat down heavily on the
bottom step and raised his open palms in a gesture of
defeat.

Shane grabbed Rhiannon's wrist. 'Let's get out of
here,' he snapped, and pulled her after him, through the
open door and down the flight of steps.

'Where's the taxi?' he asked, standing stock still for a
second in baffled rage. 'I told you to stay in it!'

'I couldn't,' she protested raggedly, her face white
with shock. 'I'll explain later.'

The gang of youths noticed their sudden appearance
and began to talk among themselves.

'The one who attacked me was with them,' said
Rhiannon, nodding her head in their direction.

Shane swore violently. 'Start running!' He pulled her
with him across the broken pavement and the unmade
road. The youths watched in surprise at their sudden

flight, but made no immediate attempt to follow. She
ran frantically beside him, her heart thudding painfully
as she fought to keep pace with his long strides. Her
high-heeled sandals were little protection from the stony
tracts of land they crossed, and with a sharp crack one
heel snapped, and she stumbled. 'I'll have to stop,' she
gasped. 'The heel's broken and my side is hurting—I
have a stitch!' She bent forward in pain.

Shane looked around them. 'We're clear now, though
heaven knows where we are. The gang were too slow off
the mark, thank goodness. It could have been nasty.'

'It *was* nasty,' she wailed, remembering the fight. 'Are
you hurt?'

Shane examined his swollen knuckles. One of his
cheekbones had been grazed, and there were spots of
dried blood on his chin, but otherwise he was intact.

'Did that bastard hurt you?' he asked in a hard voice.
She shook her head. 'Why didn't you do as I told you
to, and stay in the taxi?' he demanded, his voice rough
with anxiety. Her huge brown eyes filled with tears, and
she pulled at her trembling lower lip with her teeth.
'Forgive me, my love, please don't cry.' Shane was
immediately contrite, his arms protectively around her,
holding her close, as passers-by stared at them in curiosity. 'We must get back to the hotel. Can you manage
to walk with that broken heel, or shall I carry you?'

She smiled weakly, amused at the image of him
carrying her through the streets. 'I'm fine now,' she
assured him. 'My feet are sore, but I can manage if we
go slowly.'

They found a taxi within minutes, and were soon back
at the hotel, much to Rhiannon's relief.

Shane ran the bath and poured in a sachet of pink
crystals. 'Soak in that and bathe your feet,' he instructed
when the steaming, fragrant water was almost to the
brim. She undressed and stepped gingerly into the bath,
wincing as the hot, pink water touched raw spots on her
ankles. Then she scrubbed herself vigorously, cleaning
away the smell and feel of the youth who had attacked

her. Afterwards she closed her eyes and relaxed among the bubbles.

Shane came in and sat beside her on a stool. 'Tell me what happened,' he said, fingering her glistening shoulder. He looked grim as she explained about the driver's demands and how he had ordered her from the taxi and driven away.

'So I went into the house to look for you. The youth followed and then he made a grab for me.' She covered her face with her hands. 'It was horrible—I was so frightened!'

Tenderly he stroked the strands of damp hair at her neck until she became calm again. 'You're all right now, my love. It was my fault. I should never have taken you into such a rough area.'

'Did you discover any news of your family?' she asked. In the trauma of the struggle with the young man, and the subsequent fight, she had forgotten completely about Shane's mission.

'I met my grandfather,' he said quietly, coiling a strand of her hair around his finger. She was about to congratulate him when she saw his face. It was sombre.

'He's very old and sickly. A neighbour looks after him, and she indicated he hadn't long to live. I introduced myself as his grandson, but he was confused. He thought I was my father, and he was angry that I only spoke English.' He turned to her with a look of despair. 'He was a complete stranger, Rhi, a foreigner. He meant nothing to me. He could have been anyone. I imagined we'd be drawn together by some invisible link, but we weren't. We had absolutely no meeting point. He spat at me, and said I was too English, that I would never belong in the Philippines, that my heart was in England. He thought he was speaking to my father, but I suddenly realised how much more that applies to me. I'm a stranger here. My roots are in England, that's where I belong. I've been fooling myself all these years. I'm more English than anything else, and that's where I shall live, with you.'

Rhiannon rubbed her cheek against his, a lump in her throat. All her unspoken, half-formed fears were swept away. She drew a long breath and laughed, reaching up to kiss him in gay abandon. The frantic hours of nail-biting worry, when she had tormented herself with obscure premonitions for the future, were forgotten. The risks she had taken in persuading him to trace his family, resolve his problems, had all been worthwhile. He had, at long last, discovered where he belonged. His wanderlust was quenched. He knew now the direction he wanted to take, the life he wanted to lead—a life which placed her at its very heart.

'You'll never know how relieved I am to hear you say that,' she murmured.

'I was carried away by the romance of it all, rather like my mother,' Shane continued dryly. 'I imagined I would be able to slot in here, but I was wrong. I'd be unhappy. My discontent at being a pop star probably fuelled my restlessness, but once I'm free of Submission everything will fall into place. However, I did discover one interesting fact.' He raised a black brow. 'In his ramblings my grandfather revealed that the man Dad was supposed to have killed is alive and kicking, though not so young any more. He didn't break his skull after all. He just went home with a bad headache! Isn't it ironical—my father ruined a good part of his life, and my mother's, all for nothing. But that won't happen with you and me, my love. We'll build a good life together, for us and our children. We'll put down roots. We'll be secure—with each other, with our friends, within the community.' He stood up and started unbuttoning his shirt. 'So there we are. I shall leave Manila a much wiser man. From now on it's you and our house in Sussex for me.' He jerked his dark head. 'Move up.'

Rhiannon slid forward as he stepped naked behind her into the warm water. She leaned back, luxuriating in the feel of him against her. He kissed her ear as their bodies glided silkily together. 'How do you fancy a baby made in the Philippines,' he murmured, 'but born in England?'

When she smiled her agreement he began lathering her, making a little love until desire forced them to abandon the fragrant water and rub each other dry. Then he swung her up into his arms and carried her to the bed. His lovemaking was slow and tender. Skilfully, with infinite gentleness, he gave her pleasure until her body felt as though it was moving in a thousand different directions. He was strong and sure as he guided her towards a crescendo of ecstacy.

The time for submission was over. Shane would no longer impose his will on her. They were partners, man and wife. For ever and ever.

A WORD ABOUT THE AUTHOR

Although her first novel wasn't penned until she was nearly forty, Elizabeth Oldfield actually began writing professionally when she was a teenager. She had enrolled in a writing course taught by mail. As guaranteed, the course more than paid for itself with money she subsequently earned from sales of her writing to magazines and newspapers—but at that stage of her life, writing was really only a hobby. Soon other types of work outside the home and family life took her away from dreams of living by her pen.

After a number of years of marriage, her husband, a mining engineer, was posted to Singapore for a five-year spell. Here Elizabeth enjoyed not only exciting leisure activities—tennis, handicrafts, entertaining fascinating visitors from all over the globe—but also the opportunity to absorb as much as possible about a culture as varied as it was exotic. And having more time on her hands, she resumed her writing — once again finding success at articles, interviews and humorous pieces.

But she had a larger goal: to write a book. Romance novels caught her eye. By the time she left Singapore, she had completed two novels and eventually saw both published—sending her on her way as a romance novelist. Now she works four days a week on her books, spending the rest of her time in various activities, including, whenever possible, hours spent with her family.

LaVYRLE SPENCER
SWEET MEMORIES

a special woman...a special love... a special story

Sweet Memories is the poignant tale of Theresa Brubaker and Brian Scanlon, separated by Brian's Air Force officer training, but united in spirit by their burning love.

Alone and unsure, Theresa decides on a traumatic surgical operation that proves devastating for both her and Brian, a proud sensitive man whose feelings of betrayal run deep. Through the tears and pain, Theresa emerges from her inhibitions a passionate, self-confident woman ready to expres her love.

Harlequin Temptation

The sensuous new romance-fiction series about choices...dilemmas...resolutions...and, above all, the fulfillment of love.

These are the novels that ask your heart to decide. Because in every woman's life there comes a moment when her heart must choose her destiny.

Each of the four monthly **Harlequin Temptation** romances provides 224 pages of involving, satisfying reading entertainment for only $1.95.

Available wherever paperback books are sold or through Harlequin Reader Service:

In the U.S.
P.O. Box 52040
Phoenix, AZ 85072-2040

In Canada
P.O. Box 2800, Postal Station "A"
5170 Yonge Street
Willowdale, Ontario M2N 5T5

TEMP-1-R

THE GOLDEN CAGE

The first Harlequin American Romance Premier Edition by bestselling author ANDREA DAVIDSON

Harlequin American Romance Premier Editions is an exciting new program of longer–384 pages!–romances. By our most popular **Harlequin American Romance** authors, these contemporary love stories have superb plots and true-to-life characters–trademarks of **Harlequin American Romance**.

The Golden Cage, set in modern-day Chicago, is the exciting and passionate romance about the very real dilemma of true love versus materialism, a beautifully written story that vividly portrays the contrast between the life-styles of the run-down West Side and the elegant North Shore.

GC-3